One Break, A Thousa

One Break,
A Thousand Blows!

Maxi Kim

Semina No. 2

'[T]here are Proletarian writers who have abandoned their ideological point of view and become converted to bourgeois literature, and former bourgeois writers who joined the Proletarian ranks but who have since returned to their old roots—a wretched state of affairs indeed.'
–Kokusai Bunka Shinkokai, *Introduction to Contemporary Japanese Literature 1920–1935*

'People want to be someone.
But the really exciting challenge is to
become no one. And where will you find no ones?
In nowhere. Where things are exploding.'
–Bernadette Corporation, *Reena Spaulings*

The picture of Tomi Sasahara

The office was filled with the unusually rich fragrance of
orchids, and when the autumn breeze stirred amidst the flowers
of Chancellor Kato's greenhouse there came through the open
glass door the slightest scent of diarrhoeic dog excrement,
and the more intoxicating perfume of the sashimi-orange
mebina-hybrids.

From the northeast corner of the balcony on which he was
slouching, his left shoulder slightly higher than his right,
sipping, as was his custom, a cup of hot green tea, the
Chancellor could just catch the gleam of the honey-sweet and
honey-coloured legs of a group of post-pubescent graduate
students, whose tremulous chests seemed hardly able to bear
the burden of a beauty so flame-like as theirs; and now and then
the leaves of the chinese elms danced, accentuating the girls'
movements, elevating what looked initially like a conventional
sexual response to a scene of poignancy and trans-feminine
mystery. And as if on cue, the fantastic shadows of birds in
flight flitted across the Grand Counselor's long tussore-silk
curtains that were stretched in front of the huge sliding doors,
producing a kind of simulated japanese effect, and making him
think of those pallid, vice-addicted nineteenth century writers
of London who, through the medium of an art that is
necessarily immobile, sought to convey the sense of swiftness
and motion. The sullen murmur of water shouldering its
way through the many potted experimental breeds in the
greenhouse, or the dalmatian circling with monotonous
insistence round the dusty po-mo furniture in the sitting

room, seemed to make the stillness more oppressive. The dim roar of Tokyo was like the bourdon note of a distant organ.

In the south-west corner of the room, clamped to an upright easel, stood a full-length portrait of a girl of extraordinary beauty reclining with her legs spread, and in front of it, some little distance away, was sitting the new owner, Ryu Asakawa, whose sudden disappearance some years previously caused great public excitement and gave rise to many strange rumours. The nineteenth century picture was one of the most unusual examples of shunga, pornographic polychrome engravings painted by the Ukiyo-e school. With her bedlam of greasy hair, enigmatic stare and Egon Schiele-like composition, the print had the strange poetic expression of the genre, but none of its trappings. There are no seal marks (it is rumoured that the nihilist-haiku poet Issa had a hand in painting it), no kimono patterns, none of the formal signs of femininity. The girl is obviously a girl, but there is something tomboyish about her; or to put it as Ryu would have put it, a superhuman innocence that transcended gender.

As the academicians looked at the gracious and comely form Chancellor Kato had acquired for his long-time friend, a smile of pleasure passed across Ryu's face, and seemed set to linger there. But he suddenly started up and, closing his eyes, placed his fingers upon the lids, as though he sought to imprison within his brain some curious dream from which he feared he might awake.

'K, I want to thank you again,' said Ryu. His colleague made his way inside, took a quick glance at the black and white, near-pornographic depiction of the girl. 'Not necessary, Asakawa-san. It is I who ought to be thanking you. Do you recall the first few years? I must admit, even I had my doubts, when you initially advised the council and began to hire some of the stranger gaijin artists and curators. It was certainly a shock for our older faculty. But as you predicted, enrolment went up, cultural tourism soared, and today we have one of the premier higher education art departments in East Asia. Finding your Tomi for you was my pleasure. Of course, the trustees just about had a fit, but I'm glad I could do you the favour. It was not easy finding the dealer who had the contacts. I imagine you're going to want to show it off at the New Geisai Show?'

'I don't think I shall send it anywhere,' he answered, tossing his head back in that odd way that used to make his friends laugh at him.

'No. I won't send it anywhere.'

Chancellor Kato elevated his eyebrows; his friend had broken kata, rules of polite society. He looked at him in amazement through the thin white wreaths of steam that curled up in such fanciful whorls from his green tea. 'Not send it anywhere? But why? Have you any reason? You collectors are quite odd! I go through all the trouble of finding this one of a kind, pulling every string I had with the board. I was sure that you'd at least show it off.'

'I know you will laugh at me,' he replied, 'but I really can't show it. The sole reason I desired Tomi so desperately was so that no one else could own her.'

Chancellor Kato, an armchair horticulturist, was immediately reminded of the practice of eighteenth-century english collectors who would send men to the ends of the earth instructing them to destroy all but one of certain orchid species. The point was to skyrocket its value. The Chancellor laughed.

'Yes, I knew you would chuckle, but it is quite true, all the same.'

Ryu stood up, his back to his colleague and scanned the Chancellor's bookshelf. *Broken Silence: Voices of Japanese*

Feminism by Aoki Yayoi, Ide Sachiko, Kanazumi Fumiko and Kora Rumiko (untranslated copy). *Beauty Up: Exploring Contemporary Japanese Body Aesthetics* by Laura Miller. *Male Homosexuality in Modern Japan: Cultural Myths and Social Realities* by Mark McLelland. Ryu was the one who introduced the Chancellor to that ignoble post-1960s para-discipline.

'You misjudge me, Ryu. I have an idea of what you're trying to do. It occurred to me ever since you bought those few seventeenth-century shunga, always insisting on concealment from the general public.' It is at this point that our dear Chancellor's voice took a most highfalutin tone. 'If I'm not mistaken you're attempting to save our beautiful and innocent heroine from the everyday gaze of philistines, where the mass cloning, reproduction and dissemination of Tomi will in time seem as beautiful, if not more beautiful than the original. Yes? Believe me, Ryu, I sympathise with you. When I see the works of these hacks such as Yumiko Kayukawa or Masakatsu Sashie or any number of these young upstarts, I cringe in horror. By plagiarising, cutting and pasting, force-dovetailing the old with the new, all that is solid melts into air! They remind me of those horrid craftsmen who'd glue fragments of greek antiquities with simulated pieces fake-aged with tea. All for the sake of fast profit. And it is the same in literature today. If it isn't manga or anime, young readers are distracted by the blood and gore pulp of a Ryu Murakami or the syrupy coming of age tales of a Banana Yoshimoto. Everything holy is profaned; my students don't even have the capacity to enjoy, let alone absorb the strange clarity of Basho, the aesthetic beauty of Buson, nor the devastatingly nihilistic charms of an Issa...'

As Chancellor Kato blathered endlessly, as was his duty (in the strict Kantian sense), Ryu sensed that he would be at it for a good while. He humoured his friend and from time to time

nodded his head. Ryu's mind was somewhere else entirely.
He was of course daydreaming of his Tomi. In the fantasy
narrative, it is initially very soft, but quickly hardens in her
small, inviting hands. Within the very restrictions of the frame,
he is set free. Imagine their love nest; a warm straw-thatched
house in the middle of a bleak, barren psychogeography. From
inside one could hear the distant gruntings and songs of the
corvée labourers shouldering their faggots of wood in the bitter
cold. Any one of them would've given up their five kan in land
taxes for one night with Tomi. With both hands she strokes the
erect penis; slowly and lovingly at first, incrementally more
urgent, more violent. Ryu guides her head to his erect member,
all the while reminding her to zero in on his steely gaze. He
could see in her shimmering grey eyes, what he interpreted as
restrained _____; how he desired to unrestrain the beast
within her. He laid out the waif-like girl on the tatami mat,
pulled her legs apart, and buried his head in the furrow between
her thighs, the menstrual perfume overwhelmed his senses.
She screamed as he delved ever closer to the core of her being.
She shouts obscenities as his tongue performs minor miracles.
It is not long before she comes, our innocent shudders in
glorious rapture. A tear runs down her face as she exhales; it
is as if all of his life-energy had been forfeited for this one act
of resplendency. Tomi wants to return the favour, but he doesn't
let her. He tells her that her immediate pleasure is his concern.
She does not hesitate to comply. He wants to know all
about her.

Imagine early-eighteenth-century Edo, present day Tokyo.
According to Tomi, she was the granddaughter of the legendary
swordsman Isaburo Sasahara. How his magnificent blade
ingrained the fear of God and Buddha himself into the hearts of
his enemies. It was he who had single-handedly killed sixty-six
of his Lordship's best samurais; no blade of the Tokugawa

Regime could penetrate his lightning steel. But alas, Great Isaburo was finally taken down by dishonourable means, western gunpowder. Due to the Lordship's renewed interest in finding the fugitive granddaughter, Tomi's wet-nurse made the most difficult decision of giving away guardianship of the four-year-old Tomi to the red-faced snow monkeys of the Jigokudani clan. Normally, the two worlds never would've cooperated in such an agreement, but the snow monkeys like all in the animal kingdom had great admiration for the late Isaburo Sasahara. The slow but steady encroachment of the merchant class, corrupt Buddhist priests, and gaijin foreigners, had taken its toll on the wild; how the nippon monkeys thought fondly of the old ways; how they admired Isaburo's stand against injustice and cruel inevitability. It was certain that little Tomi would be safer in the macaque world. The vassals of the most powerful daimyo wouldn't think of looking for the girl in the freezing wasteland that was Nagano prefecture. The locals deemed it 'The Valley of Hell'. Our simian friends called it home.

As she tells her story, a series of questions occur to Ryu. *What did she eat in the mountains? How did she get along with the animal people? What was a typical day like? How did she ever get out of the clan? How did she ever manage to learn her grandfather's art of the sword? What ever prompted her to return to this world? What was the future for her?* Simultaneously, there is a weaving that occurs; a cross-pollination of his dream narrative with Chancellor Kato's pedagogical telos. But Kato's questions unlike Ryu's are simply rhetorical, ideologically driven. *Why is art today so boring? If it is the case that attitude dominates today's artmaking practice, ought we not make the case that the active feature of today's concepts and theories—those things that presumably generate art—are just mere attitudes? What business is it of career curators to contaminate the ideal utopia that is the art school? With art schools increasingly*

*functioning as extensions of museum brands, art fairs, biennials,
and the broader art market, where are the theoretical and
aesthetic hubs for the art students? Who looks out for the
emerging artist?*

To an outsider there would be something unnerving about the
way Kato went on and on. The conviction with which he spoke,
the quick, superfluous hand gestures; one wondered if he
believed even a word of it. His left eye didn't quite match up
with his right, but nevertheless he was exceptionally handsome.
Now that Ryu thinks of it, Kato was the evil twin of Toshiro
Mifune with the sculpted body of Yukio Mishima. And like the
otherworldly Mishima, he could never quite manage to bulk up
his lower half. Ryu on the other hand was of modest otaku
stock; he has been mistaken for Takashi Murakami (japan's
Andy Warhol) at a number of gallery openings.

One looks around Kato's office and it is clear that he is not
your usual conservative aesthete. Two nude paintings by Peter
McArdle. A pair of decapitated, naked black and white photos
by Gina Clark. Gifts from Ryu. Up against the mirror wall is
the couch covered with South American embroideries and
moroccan pillows. Yellow and orange flowers sit next to carved
animal sculptures and indian watercolours of elephants. What
is strange to Ryu is the lack of greco-roman and african
influence. After all, was he not an intellectual? Honestly, no one
has ever truly known the man. Ryu can't even recall where they
first met. Goldsmiths or the Jan van Eyck. Or perhaps even
CalArts. Without a doubt, it was at a lecture. Initially, Ryu truly
thought the man was like him, a nihilist. Kato had the résumé
and the flair of a Harold Bloom, but Ryu had assumed it was
all for show. An academic exercise at best. At the core of his
being, he couldn't care less. This is what Ryu told himself. It is
becoming clear to him. Even now, as Kato talks up the

debilitating aspects of contemporary culture and the horrid effects of the Bologna process, this is a man that truly believes; an ideologue who'd do almost anything for his traditionalist cause.

After a pause, Chancellor Kato pulled out his watch. 'I am afraid it is time for Chairman Mao's walk,' he murmured, 'and before I go, I insist on your answering a question I put to you some time ago.'

'What is that?' said the collector, keeping his eyes fixed on the ground.

'You know quite well.'

'I do not, Chancellor.'

'Well, I will tell you what it is. I want you to explain to me why you won't exhibit Tomi Sasahara's picture. I want the real reason.'

'I told you the real reason.'

'No, you did not. You said it was because you didn't want any one else to own it. Now, that is childish.'

'K,' said Ryu Asakawa, looking him straight in the face, 'you are right. What more do you want me to say? That the painting is not for myself? That I could not care less about the art world? And care even less about preserving Tomi's aura? Or perhaps this is the flat response that'll satisfy: the reason I will not exhibit this picture is that I am afraid that I have in it the secret of my own soul.' It was clear that Ryu was offended; you could call him almost anything, except childish. Even the mere suggestion that he was a tad naïve left him feeling painfully vulnerable. And of course, Kato knew this. He was drawing him out.

Chancellor Kato laughed. 'And what is that?' he asked.

'I will tell you,' said Asakawa; but an expression of perplexity came over his face.

'I am all expectation, Ryu,' continued his companion, glancing at him.

'Oh, there is too much to tell, Kato,' answered the collector; 'and I am afraid you will hardly understand it. Perhaps you will hardly believe it.'

Chancellor Kato smiled, and, leaning down, gave his dalmatian a sloppy kiss. 'I am quite sure I shall understand it. Isn't that right, Chairman Mao?' he replied in a playful manner. 'And as for believing things, I can believe anything, provided that it is quite incredible.'

The wind shook some blossom from the trees, and the heavy lilac-blooms, with their clustering stars, moved to and fro in the languid air. A grasshopper began to chirrup by the wall, and like a blue thread a long, thin dragonfly floated past on its brown, gauze wings. Chancellor Kato felt as if he could hear Ryu Asakawa's heart beating, and wondered what was coming.

'The story is simply this,' said the collector after some time. 'Two days ago I was giving a lecture at Kato Hall. You know we intellectuals have to show ourselves in society from time to time, just to remind the public that we are not savages. With an evening coat and a white tie, as you told me once, anybody, even an otaku, can gain a reputation for being civilised. Well, after I had been in the room about ten minutes, talking to huge overdressed PhD candidates and tedious academicians, I suddenly became conscious that someone was looking at me. I turned half-way round, and saw M. When our eyes met, I felt that I was growing pale. A curious sensation of terror came over me...'

As Ryu told the story, his grey cells could not contain the flashes of Miju. Miju's mouth probing his. Miju's moist, quivering slit. Miju's curious child gaze. Miju's scent. Miju's gasp. The way Miju pressed herself against his chest. His hands on her hips. The way Miju's small fingers snaked around his cock. Miju's restless description of the ontological similarities between Eileen Myles and Slavoj Žižek. The way Miju lit her cigarette. The way Miju playfully wagged her tongue and swallowed his cum. The seriousness with which Miju would point out the 'theoretical' difference between Sophie Calle and Chris Kraus. The way Miju would exhaustively address the fundamental nihilism that preoccupied both Allen Ginsberg and Langston Hughes. Miju climbing into bed. Miju's quirky laugh. Miju's poor-little-rich-girl act. Miju's tattooed ankle. Miju's resentment of her petit bourgeois stock. Miju's dimples. Miju's freckled bare shoulders. Miju's indignation at adopting a bourgeois sensibility. Miju's finger up my hole. Miju's high regard for japanese youth culture. The tomboyish way Miju ate watermelons. Miju's piss-stained copy of *Pirate Utopias* by Peter Lamborn Wilson (how she admired Autonomedia's Anti-copyright policy). Miju's coffee stained copy of *Why Different?* by Luce Irigaray. Miju's highlighted copy of *Soft Subversions* by Felix Guattari. Miju's dog-eared copy of *In the Shadow of the Silent Majorities* by Jean Baudrillard. But above all, her pussy farts. Miju's pussy farts. Miju's adorable pussy farts.

'A girl is a girl is a girl, Ryu. There are no real differences between this one and that one. How old are you?'

'I don't believe that, K, and I don't believe you do either. However, whatever was my motive — and it may have been pride, for I used to be very proud — I certainly struggled to the conference door. There, of course, I stumbled across M. "Hello sensai, it has been many years."'

'And what was your reply?' asked Chancellor Kato, gently stroking the dalmatian with his long, apprehensive fingers.

Ryu was absolutely stunned. Here was the former raison d'être of his life, who he presumed dead long ago, suddenly materialised out of thin air. He simply said, "Yes M, it's been too long." He stealthily manœuvred her around the graduate students, and people with stars and garters, and elderly ladies with gigantic tiaras and parrot noses. He was eager for answers, where she'd been, what she had for breakfast that morning; to catch up. But most of all, he was looking forward to being in her warm, radiant company, without any distractions. He found himself in a stolen season; he would look away for a moment and was startled to find that Miju hadn't evaporated. He found himself in her apartment— Miju suggested it. She lived near the University in an older reinforced concrete, condominium complex. Her studio apartment surprised him in that it was like nothing he had ever imagined. The floor was covered with open, marked books and ripped pages. Where was the charm? Where was the old Miju? There was no furniture. Only several tall bookcases full of tomes. He recognised some of the names. Horapollo. Sakujiro Kano. Taizo Soma. Jun Tanaka. Dai Jinhua. Dave Rimmer. Zenzo Kasai. Koji Uno. Yi In-jik. Joachim of Fiore. Paracelsus. Yi Hae-cho. Ch'oe Ch'an-shik. Kim (pronounced cheme as in scheme as Miju would later correct him) Ko-je. Seiji Tanizaki. Kazuo Hirotsu. A bloodstained Jane Austen. Sylvia Plath. Ayn Rand. Charlotte Brontë. Aby Warburg. Kathy Acker. Anne Sexton. Pauline Réage. Mary Oliver. Yuzo Yamamoto. Musoan Takebayashi. Saisei Muro. Seikichi Fujimori. A bloodstained Kiyoshi Eguchi. Hyakken Uchida. Kichiji Nakatogawa. Empedocles. Mosaku Sasaki. Masajiro Kojima. Hippocrates. Blake. Pico della Mirandola. Kyota Mizuki. Haruo Sato. A bloodstained Yuzuru Matsuoka. Masao Kume. Yoshio Tokyoshima. Kan Kikuchi. Ryunosuke Akutagawa. Michel Foucault. Claudio Ptolemy.

The books were not in alphabetical or chronological order; whatever occult organisation system she was using, Ryu had not the capacity to recognise it. Before words could even spill out of his mouth, she disrobed. She or something had managed to transform Miju in to an object. And all over her body—from the curves of her waist to the valley of her chest, were the most striking korean characters. They were not tattooed. But one could tell the ink was not new. He knew a little korean, but he could not decipher the unfamiliar hieroglyph. Almost as if he had discovered the lapis, the Philosophers' Stone itself, his hand hovered over the body of the text. And without warning, Miju's impossible lips met his. She pressed hard against him. He pressed his finger in to her celestial triangle and she squirmed with surprise. That night the couple wanted to make love in every conceivable orifice, in every possible position. But each came quickly. Could you blame them? They were making up for a dangerous length of lost time.

'I don't believe a single word you have said, and, what is more, Ryu, I feel sure you don't either. It all appears to have been culled from a postmodern novel.' The storyteller experienced a moment of mild speechlessness.

Ryu stroked his goatee, and tapped the toe of his chequerboard laced Converse Chucks with the Chancellor's tennis racket. 'Forgetful K, was it not you who said that you couldn't believe anything, unless it was quite incredible? Is it not I who tolerate your endless apologia of the East Asian world? Besides, I have not yet gotten to the most incredible aspect of that night.'

According to Miju every lost heroine had a guardian angel; hers happened to be a four-hundred-and-seventeen-year-old snow monkey of the Jigokudani clan, the anonymous, self-denying artist who had painted Tomi. He preferred to be called Yoshi. One night Miju was studying late at the library. To her surprise a small japanese macaque was attempting to read a book. He was sitting on the floor opposite her. She took note of the fact that he appeared to be a juvenile. Black eyes. Black soft fur. Red face and bottom. Short tail. Pink genitals. He had a translated copy of *A Thousand Years of Nonlinear History* by Manuel De Landa. It was a novel about everything. When she asked him if he'd enjoyed it or not, he told her he didn't know. Apparently, he came to Gakushuin Women's College Library not knowing the difference between hiragana and katakana. He told her he'd been studying for four years but he admitted he was still a slow reader. He had occasional fits of envy directed against city girls just like Miju. She noticed that he spoke with the accent of a newly arrived foreigner from the states. He told her his name was Yoshitomo.

That night she earned Yoshi's trust and he revealed to her that his profoundest desire was to write a novel like her stepfather. Apparently, this was the reason why he had taken such risks to find her. When she asked him what genre piqued his interests, he said he wanted to write like Ryu Murakami. But with more pornographic possibilities and subterfuge. Personally, she didn't think anyone could imitate this style; but she encouraged the snow monkey nonetheless. She had a fair amount of respect for writers who could conjure up a good sex scene. Hence, her attachment to Mister Trippy. She told him she too wanted to write a novel. About japan. But then again who didn't? The protagonist was to be a metaphor. The metaphor wanted to negate japan, but not by *not* writing a novel about japan, but by writing falsely about it, using japan as a screen for the author's innermost hopes and desires. It is not only in poetry where we metaphoricise; when a baby sexualises a pacifier as if it was the mother's nipple—is this not metamorphosis at its most literal? She wanted to express the claim that there was no gap between sexuality and textuality. This was her aim. And she only called it a novel because she didn't know what else to call it at the time.

Yoshi's aim was anti-metaphorical. He told her that the point
was to get past modernism, get past postmodernism. To express
a pre-modernist, posthuman morphogenetic aesthetics in all
its wild and sacred expressivity. She told him his project was
perverse. He smiled. The monkey then asked if she would
help him with his book. She told him she would, but on one
condition. He would have to give her something in return.
He told her that he would help her uncover the truth about
her mother. She said no. He then offered to tell her where her
biological father was. She agreed. Little did she know that he
meant her 'literal' father as in the Latin litteralis 'of or belonging
to letters or writings'. Still, this was of no real concern. He
knew what she knew; who she really wanted to meet was her
phantasmatic Other. You see, like Ryu she was suffering from
spiritual syphilis.

The sheer irreducibility of Gina Clark

For the emerging artist, the question is EVERYTHING. *Who am I? Which artist ought I imitate? Amy Adler? Malerie Marder? CHRISTINE WERTHEIM? Michael Craig-Martin? John Baldessari? Thomas Hirschorn? JON WAGNER? Maria Martinez-Canas? Matthew Barney? NORMAN KLEIN? Kara Walker? Atsuko Tanaka? Lu Jian Jun? Gilbert & George? Gerard & Daiana? Another YBA? Ryan Gander? Salomon Huerta? Ray Johnson? Robert Longo? RYU ASAKAWA? GINA CLARK? David Salle? CINDY SHERMAN? CECILY BROWN? Danielle Adair? Jenny Holzer?*

CHRISTINE WERTHEIM? In Janine's dream narrative she is swapping spit with the australian headmistress. They are out on the sloping lawn adjacent to the Chouinard Hall dormitory. Embraced, they roll down spinning:

WEEEEEEEEEeeeeeeeeEEEEEEEEeeeeeeEEEEEEEeee eee EEEEeeeeEEEEeeeeeeee!!! Janine's face buried in her two overripe melons. She twined her legs around her so that their genitals could meet and rub through the wool. At the bottom, they find each other covered with hickies and grass stains. Christine laughs and tells Janine how much fun she's having. They dry hump. The young artist found herself about to ejaculate. They want to prolong this need. They grow bored. They circle the campus and Janine asks the former professor of Goldsmiths College about the ideal setting for art education. It is her idea that it ought to be modelled after hyperbolic spaces, creative interspaces. She references Kant, Melville, and mathematical models. Because she isn't canonically-read and calculus-literate, it is difficult for Janine to follow. But the simple crux of the argument appears to depend on the 'un-institutionalising' of the institution: to undo all the harm done by Margaret Thatcher, to give back the autonomy that art schools once had prior to the eighties and nineties. Of course, so many conservatives are afraid of 'un-institutionalising' because they see it synonymous with 'no institution'. But as Allan Kaprow's ghost would insist, there is a big difference between being an 'un-artist' and not being an artist at all. Or as Christine would put it, the non-classical gap between the 'not-dressed' and the 'undressed'. Or as Žižek so marvellously put it, the gap between the 'not-dead' and the 'undead'. Think Stephen King.

CINDY SHERMAN? *'One thing I've always known is that the camera lies.'* Wigs, prosthetics, haute couture! What could be more amusing? More carnal? More post-feminist? CECILY BROWN? *The Girl Who Had Everything. Hard, Fast and Beautiful.* Flashiest of pinks. Her traumatised, Michael Jackson complexion, literally dripping with sex. Seamlessly more carnal, more post-feminist. The only thing that bothered Janine about Brown was her use of paint. She couldn't see her self in front of a canvas. All that negative white space. *Smooth, flaky whiteness.* If only someone could relieve Janine's doubts. Put her genius mind at ease. Out of the one thousand or so art students hurdling aimlessly through CalArts, Janine Kitani was one of the handful that would make it. *This was the false telos Janine was so desperately invested in.* Within a decade her defiant pose would be on the cover of *ARTFORUM*, *ARTnews* and *MODERN PAINTERS*. Her text-based media art included in many of the world's bienniales: Venice, The Whitney. Particularly influential in São Paulo. And it wasn't because she had the keenest eye or the best talent, nor was she the most photogenic. It was her degree of self-knowledge, the highest of any artist you've ever met. By the time she graduated CalArts an uncanny METAMORPHOSIS was to occur. She'd legally change her name back to Miju, mentally catalogue all her vulnerabilities, all her Machiavellian strengths. Our heroine understood precisely what her motivations were; subconscious and otherwise. *Wouldn't be above licking cunt and sucking cock to get ahead.* The self-described 'half-japanese, enfant terrible of Los Angeles' would hone an unscrupulous cunning, a scary knack for getting others to do for her what she herself didn't have the skill or energy for. Give her enough time and Miju Kitani could take over the world.

But this 'pouty-lipped, cigarette dangling from her fingertips' version of herself was a long way off. She was still Janine, a second-year BFA art student toying with the idea of painting. Could you imagine? Mousy, wiry Janine in an over-sized smock or a ridiculous pair of denim overalls, above the Main Gallery? In one of the Mezzanine studios? Her lifeless black mane tied in a pony tail. Her nervous, shimmering grey eyes turned dark by the impossibility of all that paint. BLUE CHINA ASTER! ORANGE NEW DAHLIA ROOTS! BARE BOTTOMED MACAQUE RED! LICORICE PURPLE! FLUORESCENT YELLOW BANANA YOSHIMOTO! IKEBANA GREEN! *I AM NOT POLLOCK! I'm just not. The time my father pushed me in to the pool; I almost drowned. The panic—all in the name of instruction. 'Pale waters, paler cheeks, where'er I sail.'* To be pulled in to terror where the task necessitated one to tame and challenge a white monolith, that iceberg faced nothingness! *'The marble pallor lingering there; as if indeed that pallor were as much like the badge of*

consternation in the other world, as of mortal trepidation here…
all ghosts rising in a milk-white fog.' Alien. Indifferent. Janine
was right to intuit that she'd fail as a painter.

NORMAN KLEIN? In Janine's fantasy narrative the author
of *The History of Forgetting* drills his prick into her bum.
*EEEEEEEEEeeeEEEEEEeeeeeeeEEEEEeeeEEEEEeeeEE
EEeeeEEEEEeeeeeEEEEEEEEEEEEEEEEEE!!!* As the
media historian filled her insides with his spunk, Janine hung on
tightly to the rail of the balcony and looked out at the parking
lot adjacent to the Butler Building. A crowd was forming: Beth,
Bradley and Dante looked up in astonishment. Ten minutes in,
her asshole was desperately sore and her backside was on the
verge of welting from Klein's brute, successive slaps. He
finished with a low moan. And she could feel the hot discharge
bubbling out of her backdoor fun-hole. To both of their
chagrin, a sudden roar of applause from below. The three had
multiplied into thirty-three. There were Beth's friends: Molly
and Honey, Allison, Gerard and Daiana. Bradley's friends:
Daniel and David. Dante's friends: Joe and Uncle Joe. Their
faces grew red. In a blur, Norman, with his pants around his
ankles, staggered to the restroom to get the shit off his fuck
stick. Janine hiked up her skirt and ran in the opposite direction.
She was late for her friend's installation-performance.

She couldn't believe it. Gina Clark had managed to transform
the usually quiet and brightly lit, white Stevenson Blanche
Gallery into the performance artist's site of ritual and renewal.
The entirety of the space was covered in dirt and lit with a single
candle. Recorded audio of trains passing by Clark's home set
the mood. Fastened to the walls one could see photographic
documentation of Clark's previous performances. One in
particular caught Janine's eye. Titled *Incident, Memory and the
Myth*, it was a twenty-by-twenty-four-inch large black and

white, bird's eye view photo of the rope-bound torso of a decapitated, 'undressed' and aroused female body—Gina Clark's body. Here was the final expression of the postmodern deadlock, Janine thought. As of late she'd been reading *The Fragile Absolute* by Slavoj Žižek. According to the Marxist-Lacanian, 'Gustave Courbet's (in)famous *L'origine du monde*, the torso of a shamelessly exposed, headless, naked and aroused female body, focusing on her genitalia; this painting, which literally vanished for almost a hundred years, was finally […] the reversal of the sublime object into abject, into an abhorrent, nauseating excremental piece of slime […] Courbet's gesture is thus a dead end, the dead end of traditional realist painting— but precisely as such, it is a necessary "mediator" between traditional and modernist art—that is to say, it represents a gesture that *had to be accomplished* if we were to "clear the ground" for the emergence of modernist "abstract" art'.

For Ryu *Incident* was not only the gesture that *had to be accomplished* if we were to 'clear the ground' for the emergence of post-postmodernist 'unabstract' art, but it was an incommunicable mirror that had somehow captured the newly emerging paracultural spirit of the short twenty-first century. Think of Brutalism, Stuckism, and Neoism; the enigmatically raw prose-poetics of Adelle Stripe, the curious postgallery nude paintings of Peter McArdle, and the energetic punk pranksterism of Mister Trippy. But the uk art scene wasn't always so inviting. London had initially been very cruel to Ryu. Although he greatly appreciated the fact that many of London's major museums were free to enter, the speed of the city began to take its toll on him. He was reminded of something Norman Klein had written in his little black book *Freud in Coney Island and Other Tales*, 'In the late nineteenth century, millions of people suffered from neurasthenia. It was the culturally apt disease of its time. Its symptoms were brought on by excessive

modernity (quite vague symptoms at that, one size fits all).
Weber had it. Bergson had it. So did William James, Dreiser,
Edith Wharton, Proust'. Perhaps excessive postmodernity
was Ryu's problem. He was fatigued, depressed by all the
neocorporate neoconceptualism. The ybas didn't impress him
so much. Their work was always too shiny, it hurt his eyes.
Fifty million pound-migraine pains. And then one day he found
himself in Highgate Cemetery. The stone angels and ivy set the
mood, but he was really there to see Karl Marx's grave. A
penetrating homesickness torched his department store palate.

Of course, it would've crossed anyone's mind. Rather than
aggressively attacking the void, perhaps she could befriend it.
Compliment it. Become the imperial hue's empress. *Like Agnes
Martin*. 'Agnes Martin reminds us how much can be expressed
with (seemingly) so little.' Swept by the daydream, she pulled
out her red composition book and began to write sincerely.
Naively. *Oh, / Oh Agnes, / Oh Agnes Martin / Your age does
nothing but endear you / Your straight but 'not straight' lines. /
The horizontal 'lines' of it all / Never vertical for it's never too
'strong' / The hint of imperfection creeps through the canvas. /
Reminds me of the tides in Monterey. / Scent of deep sea oceans.
/ Salty as hell. / The RUSH of tides Crashing off / Monterey
rocks. / Residual sounds of tidal waves. Incoherent. / THE
BLINDING VISION OF RICH BLUE WATERS. /
VIEWING THE SENSATIONS OF SUN-LIGHT
REFLECTIONS BOUNCING OFF THE 'ACTIVENESS'
of the vast, vast sea…* Stopstopstopstopstopstopstopstop-
stopstop! Fortunately, a grey-cell sparked and then nine
progressively milder ones. She had slipped into the old trap.
And Janine's face grew red. *What am I doing? The world
doesn't need another Agnes Martin! Not another!* And for
that matter—the world didn't need another Cindy Sherman
(although, arguably, the world would've happily

accommodated a Cindy 2). *WHAT AM I DOING IN ART SCHOOL? (What am I doing with my life?)* – she wrote melodramatically in block letters *(and then cursive)* along the top margin. The young artiste was supposed to be having the time of her life. No one tells you the second year is the worst. It had been seven months from her dorm to classes and to parties and from parties to her dorm and back to classes. Her aura slowly resembling Esther Greenwood's. She can well imagine her doe eyes welling up. She was close to the bottom. It had occurred to Plath's doppelgänger she had to reconsider the question of artistry. Reconsider her RAISON D'ETRE. Reconsider EVERYTHING. As if she was another saccharine character in a rape-revenge narrative, the Miju-to-be was due for what one of her professor's called the ultimate 'Joycean literary concept—that of the epiphany, the moment of authentic insight that marks several of the short stories in *The Dubliners*'.

The waif-like bundle of nerves in the academe-green velvet jacket hurried past the reception desk and the corporate list of financial donors in the main foyer. The hideous, iron-circle sculpture placed near the front steps to welcome prospective artists, writers, dancers, filmmakers, musicians and actors only sparked in her the realisation that her future at California Institute of the Arts was uncertain. Would she join the short list of notable CalArts alumni and happy dropouts? Tony Oursler (BFA 79). Eric Fischl (BFA 72). Barbara Bloom (BFA 72). Mike Kelly (MFA 78). Stephen Prina (MFA 80). David Salle (BFA 73, MFA 75).

Or would she join the dishearteningly long list of not-so-notable CalArts alumni? Those who never had any discernible talent. Or those who could not stomach Cowboy Bill's critique sessions. Or those who were either stifled prematurely by circumstance or simply too frightened to meet that grand canyon-gulf between what an artist was in his or her miserable, stupid reality and what he or she could've been, ought've been—*only in dreams*. Karen Eliot. Reena Spaulings. bell hooks. Luther Blissett. Alex Brener. Istvan Kantor. Gina Pun. Ed Earl. Art Vatinkson. Amy N. Bather. Javier Ruiz. Amber Bream. Nova Tarnkits. Van U. Shodlirere. Dave Russells. Artemus Barnoza. T. Emin. B. Jorofksy. Marcus Morris. Yah S. Kim. L. Baldementi. S. Iketani and Nobuko Yoshiyo and Chiyo Unoa and Kokuseki Oizumia and D. Hirst and Kiku Aminoa and Ken (Takeru) Inuk and Kosaku Takii and H. Fromm and F. Fukuyama and Norm Brown and Yuriko Chu and S. Ozaki and D. Walters and Chiako Shimomura and Bill McGonagal and M. Craig-Martin and Shinichi Makino and B. Fukunaga and Delphine B. and Jitsuzo Shiraishi and Genkichi Hosoda and Tamiki Hosodao and S. Okada and David Bae and L. Clout and K. Mizumori and Bouvard and Pécuchet and T. Kato and Sakujira Kano and R. Whiteread and Jun Tanaka and F. Picabia and M. Ray and Yoshimi 3 and Yoshimi 2 and Kojie Uno and Seiji Tanizake and Kazuo Hirotsua and Y. Yamamoto and R. Deckard and M. Takebayashi and Saisei Muroe and Seikichi Fujimorie and Kiyoshi Eguchie and Kim Devlin and Hyakken Uchida and Kichije Nakatogawa and M. Zych and Mosakuu Sasaki and M. Kojima and A. Wilson and M. Duchamp and Haruo Satu and Yuzuru Matsuoku and R. Mita and Masao Kuma and S. Marquess and Sean Moxley and Yoshio Toyoshimo and _____.

Many dull corpses in the school's coffers. Her head was spinning, contemplating all those anonymous names that came before her; the names set her pulse racing. And it wasn't simply the volume—it was the high, unrelenting speed at which they attacked her nervous system. Ticktickticktickticktickticktick. One right after the other. No time to empathise with any of them. Perhaps this is what all those french theory books meant. To be post-human. To have her name follow Jack Goldstein's. This would've been an act of grace from the universe, an astonishment. Janine needed some air. She moved beyond the long walkway and claustrophobic front entryway, and into the large main parking lot adjacent to the acres of lush emerald green; at night you could see the underground population of bashful bunnies and people-friendly squirrels copulating. Awkward young art students making out in front of Chouinard and Ahmanson Halls. The chinese elms, eucalyptus, pine and oleander—all swayed in unison as if to an unheard melody and occasionally broke off as if to a John Cage nonmelody. The clean April winds whipped through the sixty acres overlooking the incorporated nightmare city of Santa Clarita. The New World Order was just as Philip K. Dick had described it. There was no architecture. No culture. No future. The town centre was a pedestrianised shopping nightmare. Concrete! Strip malls!! Urban sprawl!!! The whole affair was uninspired. Everything was designed to move neither the intellect nor spirit. Everyone however considered the campus a consolation, an oasis in a lifeless desert.

Built with Disney money in the 1970s, the boxy, unfinished four-floor maze of playhouse laboratories had inspired a slew of writings. It was practically a cottage industry. The different literary approaches to CalArts were as eclectic as the students who attended. Writers such as David Antin wrote more or less fondly about the Institute while theoreticians like Sande Cohen (a faculty member with his share of enemies) took a more critical approach. The most approachable book on the subject was probably Mark Norris' *Art School*. Three hundred pages of what it was like to be a depressed, down-and-out twenty-four-year-old student at 'California Contemporary Arts' in 1979. More entertaining than Chip Kidd's *Cheese Monkeys*. More honest than Terry Zwigoff's *Art School Confidential*. The second most notable (if not the most influential) 'Calle Arts' book was of course Chris Kraus' scandalous *I Love Dick*, a book about 'her' obsession with the long-time Critical Studies Dean, Dick _____. But of course, the terrible schism with the release of the book. Not everyone was happy; Allucquere (rumoured to be the proxy leader of the Bernadette Corporation) was close with _____, and his leaving marked a psychic vacuum that could never be filled by interim so and so's. With that and *Video Green: Los Angeles Art and The Triumph of Nothingness*, Kraus had permanently etched her name in CalArts lore. This was one of the things that attracted adventurous students like Janine and lecturers like Ryu to the school. All of the wild anecdotes, fiction and mythology that maintained the impossible, but nonetheless consistent Art School cognitive mapping or psychogeography —it hearkened back to what Janine had highlighted only two days prior on page seven of Christian Bok's *Pataphysics The Poetics of an Imaginary Science*, 'Borges in Tlon, Uqbar, Orbis Tertius imagines an allegory about the seductions of simulation. A secret cabal of rebel artists has conspired to replace the actual world, piece by piece, with a virtual world, so that the inertia of a true history vanishes, phase by phase, into the amnesia of a false memory.'

Circling the campus had helped. Janine's art star anxieties had evaporated with the steady sight of the surrounding Tehachapi Mountains to the north, the lines of the San Gabriels cutting across the sky to the east and the distant Santa Susannas to the west. Her mind wandered as her iPod went through a personal soundtrack. *Rebel Girl* by Bikini Kill. *Art Star* by Yeah Yeah Yeahs. *What's Yr Take On Cassavettes* by Le Tigre. *Revolt* by Lesbians on Ecstasy. *Punk Girl* by Thee Headcoatees. *Judy Is A Punk* by Ramones. *Eating Toothpaste* by Bratmobile. *Friends & Goal* by Thug Murder. *Our Time* by Yeah Yeah Yeahs.

Plainsong by The Cure. *Who or what could possibly inhabit those heights? Lizard Kathy Acker men? Private armies ready to unleash their fury on 2012? The return of Quetzalcóatl?* She was ready to re-enter the world. Luckily, for her Tatum Lounge was open. D213 was a coffee bar located more or less at the back-end of the Institute. The espresso wasn't so hot and the fluorescent lighting wreaked havoc, but the crowd was smarter, less invested in pretentiousness than the Starbucks on McBean Parkway.

Young Folks by Peter Bjorn and John was playing and slumped over in a corner with his iBook was Ryu Asakawa. Usually his black eyes withdrew so suspiciously under their brows. Here was a misanthropist just as sickly and thin as Janine. As a kind of Otaku she admired Ryu's beige suede and tangerine CLOT Air Max sneakers. Probably wearing art-black, he could've passed as Takashi Murakami's morose son. He resembled a monkey, a cute monkey at that.

The intricate corruption of a Tokyo girl's head

My name is Miju Kitani. I like to have sex. And I enjoy reading books. But I'm a horrible poet because I like to exaggerate fashionably. Ever since I was a suckler of my stepmother's teat I've wanted to abandon the haiku, a tiny verse-form in favour of straightforward prose narrative. It's longer. And apparently easier. And my stepfather tells me that my haiku-poems are 'much too indulgent', always lacking in pretence and metaphorical clarity. I'd like to change all that. But it's not because I take his criticisms personally. I don't. And I try not to be offended. He is an artist after all. And all artists have big dicks. He must know what he's talking about. He reminds me that I lack the philosophical awareness of a great haiku writer and poet like Basho (1644–1694). And Basho had a significant sex. I will never attract Basho's genius. I don't have the artistic craftsmanship of Buson (1715–1788). Buson of course was rumoured to have housed a six-inch snake. And according to my stepfather I've lived much too happy of a privileged, Tokyo girl life to know anything substantial about the morose sadness and nihilism of a great haiku poet like Issa (1763–1827). Later on I discovered Issa was the exception to the rule. A few artists have small dicks. But he's right. I was silly to ever think I could be an accomplished poet. It is not in my nature to be succinct. And how can I argue with my stepfather? He is an accomplished artist after all. Artists have big dicks. Unstable narratives are my niche.

You didn't always want to burn books. There was a time—
before you became well-acquainted with Professor Asakawa,
before you had to commute to Tokyo, before you got accepted
into your mother's University when the thought of dousing
paperbacks in kerosene and then igniting it—never would've
even crossed your mind, let alone fill you with such sexual
pleasure and adrenaline (as it did right now).

Yet here you were (your panties wet) on top of holy Fuji-san
with the tired and balding Professor Asakawa, standing on the
peak of a pile of overdue library books. You don't even bother
to ask how he ever managed to lug it all to the top of Mt. Fuji.
He must've befriended graduate students. There must be at least
a thousand paperbacks. You note the authors that are about to
be cremated. You are vaguely familiar with most of the names.

Shinzaburo Iketani. Nobuko Yoshiya. Chiyo Uno. Kokuseki
Oizumi. Kansuke Naka. Kiku Amino. Ken (Takeru) Inukai.
Kosaku Takii. Yuriko Chujo. Shiro Ozaki. Chiaki Shimomura.
Jiro Sekiguchi. Shinichi Makino. Banka Fukunaga. Jitsuzo
Shiraishi. Genkichi Hosoda. Tamiki Hosoda. Saburo Okada.
Murao Nakamura. Kamenosuke Mizumori. Takeo Kato.
Sakujiro Kano. Taizo Soma. Jun Tanaka. Zenzo Kasai. Koji
Uno. Seiji Tanizaki. Kazuo Hirotsu. Yuzo Yamamoto. Musoan
Takebayashi. Saisei Muro. Seikichi Fujimori. Kiyoshi Eguchi.
Hyakken Uchida. Kichiji Nakatogawa. Mosaku Sasaki.
Masajiro Kojima. Kyota Mizuki. Haruo Sato. Yuzuru
Matsuoka. Masao Kume. Yoshio Toyoshima. Kan Kikuchi.
Ryunosuke Akutagawa.

What Professor Asakawa was doing was wrong. You being a
witness to it was wrong. Maybe you didn't know it at the
time—standing on the summit—above the morning cloud layer,
breathing in the thin air, your fingers frostbitten, your legs and

shoulders aching, your back to Fuji-san's smouldering crater, your front to the smouldering paper pile—but you knew it in your last year at the University. If your memory is to be trusted it started in winter semester. A chance meeting with a leaflet. You saw it outside the Humanities building—stapled to the bulletin board. It read:

Literature Colloquium Series:
"Ideology and Misrepresentation
of the 20th century Novel Genre"
3:00pm—5:00pm.
Location: Kato Lecture Hall
Category: Lecture by Ryu Asakawa.
Open to: Public
Admission: Free

The ceiling of Kato Lecture Hall is high above you. And the wall closest to you is entirely made up of a special glass. It prevents people from the outside looking in, allowing only people on this side of the glass to look inside-out. Why the building designer was allowed to include such an extravagance is unimaginable. The rest of the walls are constructed out of translucent steel beams (unheard of outside of Tokyo) and transparent green glass. It successfully created the illusion you were in a much more spacious hall than was actually the case. It is a self-consciously postmodern piece of architectural design. Toyo Ito's wet dream.

It's been four years at the university and you've sat and listened and slept through over three-dozen lectures in Kato Lecture Hall. But none was more fascinatingly indecipherable or as personally debilitating than Professor Asakawa's notorious lecture entitled 'Ideology and Misrepresentation of the 20th

century Novel Genre'. You remember it vividly. You were on
the rag. And you were fortunate enough to have brought along
your stepfather's recorder. The batteries dying, so you only
managed to record the first half. But it's still a find considering
that you own the only known audio-recording.

He begins sanely enough. 'japanese literature [knowing pause]
is in a state—a state similar to which gaijin literature finds itself
in today—a state of crises, a state of chaos, and consequently
a state of disrepair. From my estimation it's been in this
predicament for over a decade with no discernable end in sight.
And what won't solve it—I can assure you—is looking to the
new west. Gaijin entertainers will not victimise the japanese lay
person any longer. In the next hour or so I will outline for the
incredulous listener why this is the case—why the twentieth
century novel genre as we know it today as academicians is for
all intents and purposes—dead. Consequently, I suspect that
many of you who have invested so much of your professional
careers, so much of your energy, so much of your concerted
life-force to the monster-monolith that is literary criticism
will come out of this lecture feeling a bit defeated, drained.
Perhaps disillusioned. Good! That is the point. As your
illustrious Chancellor has adroitly noted, my name is in fact
R. Asakawa. Most of you will know me as M.T. Hokusai,
the pseudonym used for my book *The Eastern Canons*
[applause]—a tome that despite your feigned accolades is I'm
sure secretly despised by all juniors who've had the misfortune
of having to take my seminar on *Buddhistic Medieval
Literature* [laughter].'

Five years' separation had changed him. You ask who is this
man? Where is the naive boy you so frantically fell in love with?
If he saw you now would he even recognise you? Remember
your name? Your sweet Ryu had become a fire-engine-red

nationalist, a mean one at that. What he needed was a full-frontal snogging!! Although he was not physically intimidating like a Mishima, his speech contained all of the tell-tale signs, the trappings of a dumb conservative. No more facial hair. No more fun. You begin to reassess the past. If a person believes in one thing and then suddenly believes in the complete opposite—what does that mean? Where is the real 'real'? Some people would claim that Ryu never truly believed in the original thing. Nor would I say the old thing was a mask for the kernel of truth, this new thing. Or vice versa. No! I think we should be bold enough to claim that the fact that one can be a believer today and an atheist tomorrow is nonsense; what that really means is that the two are closely linked. Of course, I would not go as far as to say that they are the same. But just as black and white, superego and id, god and devil are one—perhaps old Ryu and new Ryu shared an excess, a blinding void that went beyond stuffy theory and the minutiae of culture.

You recall the first time you spent some time with Ryu. It was at Gina Clark's 'Stephenson Blanche' performance. There she was with her sister Jaime. They were both 'undressed' as a Christine Wertheim might've spat. Eyes closed, both are in a trance. Their spontaneous movements cause the flame of the candle to skip and pop. They cover their exposed bodies with a sensuous mix of beans, flour, and egg yolks. Clark's crotch tainted with bits of beet. A flood of associations follow: David Lynch's wet dream? Matthew Barney's wet dream? Yours? Mine? Jack Goldstein's? What heightens the mood? The sound of trains passing: pained. Spiritual. Why does this make me feel traumatised? But I'm not sad. Could there be such a thing as happy trauma? The body as the ultimate site of the incident? Or as Paul Virilio might say, 'the accident'? Baldessari's 'situation'? The reflection of the light. It was so beautiful. The audience could barely make out the signs on Gina's right arm. The tattoos of transcendent blue clouds, a green humming bird, and countless alien eyes. Witnessing Clark and sister Jamie play with *inanimate nourishment*, attentive viewers could not help but make psychic connections with *Dimensions of Dialogue*, the delirious 1982 stop-motion film by czech surrealist Jan Švankmajer. If there is a post-postmodernism to be had, perhaps it will be a kind of surrealism.

And then we see the first, unmistakable signs of his sanity slowly eroding away into that soft, gelatinous ether academicians know as the Fuji-no-Yamabiraki. 'I don't know how many of you got to the last chapter of *The Eastern Canons* but if you have read it, you'll now hear it again. There is hope for literary studies in the twenty-first century. Unlike my balding gaijin contemporary, I see deconstructionists, feminists, Lacanians, Marxists, new historicists, and semioticians not as the six branches of the school of resentment but as the six branches of the school of salvation. If one is looking for salvation from the dead formalism of pompous, old coots— sexually crazed and from Yale no doubt—go ahead and read your Ralph Waldo Emerson. Go hide under Henry James' rotting corpse. Sodomise Thoreau. Sodomise Whitman at will. Ejaculate all over the browned pages of *Moby Dick* and we will see who is saved. We will see who trembles under the bright lights.'

The new Ryu had faith in postmodern theory. Imagine the new library: Karl Marx's *18th Brumaire of Louis Bonaparte*. Derrida's *Of Grammatology* (Translated by Gayatri Chakravorty Spivak). Cornel West's *Race Matters*. *French Theory in America,* edited by Sylvère Lotringer and Sande Cohen. The old Ryu despised them all. What could account for the gap? It was after Gina's show. We were outside drinking some cheap cabernet. I was horny and so was Ryu. Karaoke room anyone? A lot of the too-cool-for-school kids didn't get Gina's performance. Too messy. Too gnarly. Too much. They didn't have the naïveté, the necessary zero-level to see the positive emancipatory potential of the body. They were too hung up on their attitudes. Students of bell hooks thought Clark's performance was intrinsically too binary, too exploitative of the body. What they had singularly failed to do was to give up the postmodern ghost. At every level today, is there not a return to the zero level? Feminism's return to First Wave practices? A return to philosophical discourse as Socrates first intended with the popularity of YouTube? The popularity of Žižek? In an enigmatic way the best symbol for this levelling is the World Trade Center! Could we not say that the levelling of the double, the binary, means the end of simulation? Is this not the true symbolic value of Clark and her sister's accident? In Baudrillard's book the World Trade Center is *the* symbol. Can we not say that the negation of this symbol is a return to the Real? The Real of History? Fuck Francis! And fuck all you knee-jerk students of Hegel!!!

As an otaku, what I despise about orthodox feminism (even the highly ironic, highly sophisticated mutations such as Donna Haraway's) is its total inability to engage with japanese Youth culture. Take for example, Aeon Flux. Peter Chung is for me the premiere CalArts graduate. However you try and elaborate complex philosophical notions (such as mind-body dualism, intercorporeality, Phantasy, the void, etc) using the coordinates provided by Aeon Flux and the students of bell hooks invariably deride you. Right away it is asserted that anime is *inherently* obscene, *intrinsically* negative in its emancipatory potential. They point to all the dead bodies; the mountain of light blue corpses found in the Liquid TV shorts. But wait a minute! Don't feminists actively use a mountain of corpses? Don't they actively manipulate naked bodies? What about the

flood of bare-breasted women on the cover of the recent
WACK! catalogue? Why is it boldly explicit, an ironic critique
when the Museum of Contemporary Arts does it? And why
is it brutal commercial exploitation when an ex-student of
CalArts does it? The gap between the two may be shorter than
you think. Is it not MOCA that is currently showcasing the
work of Takashi Murakami? Is there actually a substantial gap
between this japanese otaku and that other, less acclaimed
korean-born otaku?

An art dealer, an art critic, and an art student—all go to an art
opening at a prominent school. In the main gallery there's a
mirror with the word NAÏVE across it. The dealer looks at it
for a second, can't see a place for it in the marketplace and
dismisses it. The critic looks at it for a second, sees it as another
sophomoric attempt at postmodern irony and quickly dismisses
it. The art student lingers in front of the piece as she uses the
mirror to redo her mascara and fix her hair. You get the joke?
Of course, for many the message here is that the art student
is the most naïve; this is a joke about the art student's lack
of awareness and theoretical sophistication. But what if the
message of the joke is the opposite one? Namely, that it is the
dealers and the critics who don't get it; and perhaps they are
the most naïve. If we are to take seriously the emancipatory
potential of 'everyday art' à la Joseph Beuys and Allan Kaprow,
isn't the most sublime gesture a utilitarian one? If we truly want
to obliterate the distinction between art and life; to essentially
deprivilege, dethrone the category of art—ought we not
dethrone the role of the market? Dethrone the role of theory??
Become naïve???

'Without the help of deconstruction. Without the help of
feminists, new historicists, semioticians—you can only go so far
into the world of literature. Even if you call yourself a formalist

this is meaningless if you can't decipher something as extensive and as complex as James Joyce's *Ulysses*. Anyone who claims you can understand *Ulysses* simply by reading it is insane. One must analyse complexities, not distil them and drink them as if it was the whore geisha's saki. But don't get me wrong. I am not saying don't read the classics. I do not support The Campaign to Abolish The Complete Works of William Shakespeare. What I am saying is that using methodologies such as deconstruction is the best way to read Emerson, James, Thoreau, Whitman, and Shakespeare—and that this is preferable to the nonsensical ideology of those who claim that Emerson, James, and Shakespeare are somehow beyond the realm of critical, societal analysis and commentary. Those who insist the western canons are supposedly god-sent and divinely inspired and not to be questioned are talking rubbish. Fragmentation is the key. Madness, literal madness is what I want.'

That night Ryu and I made out in the parking lot. The performance had jumpstarted our libidos. CalArts had a stretch of lawn adjacent to the car park. It was perfect for two things: day dreaming and dry humping. We quickly grew bored of safe sex, and Ryu decided to eat me out. He lapped up the discharge of oil-like blood and mucosal tissue from my uterus. I could tell that the aroma was pungent by Ryu's amusing expressions. I told him his ministrations weren't necessary, but he knew my secret desire was his ransacked tongue. *Turning and turning in the widening gyre / The pirat cannot hear the piratas; / Things fall apart; the centre cannot hold; / Mere attitude is loosed upon the world, / The blood-dimmed hurrikan is loosed, and everywhere / The ceremony of meaning is drowned; / The best lack all conviction, while the worst / Are full of passionate intensity. / Surely some revelation is at hand; / Surely a post-post modernism is at hand.*

Once Ryu had unloaded his love juice all over my chest, we lay
there in the grass. Pointed out constellations; made up some
new ones. And both of us took a few drags. It was very windy
that night; very spooky. I told him a story about my
grandmother; how she came home one day from work. She
shat in the backyard. The dog tried to eat it. He dragged a stick
through it. And made a wonderful mess. He told me the story
of how his pet rat got out of its plastic cage. He found it in
one of those gooey mouse motels. His mum had to break its
neck. Sooner or later we got around to talking about Gina's
performance. We both agreed. The students of Derrida were
complete idiots. Deconstructionists—especially the ones
around the University of California circuit—had a line on
rhetorical questioning that was quite superfluous. They could
not entertain the possibility that *Incident, Memory and the
Myth* (Stevenson Blanche Gallery, March 2006), *Arms Become
Cabinets, Eyes Remain Stones* (D301, November 2006) *and
Flicking the Tit of the Weeping Lemur* (Stevenson Blanche
Gallery, April 2007) represented answers, not questions.
Enigmatic meaning arrived as an answer. Now what was
the question?

'…and the solution to today's passive nihilism is a return,
a resurrection of the most basic kind. In the west's case, it is
a return to painting as the so-called "new old masters" have
shown. From the broad steel-panelled floral still lifes of the
recently deceased David Bierk to Julie Heffernan's fruit-and-
animal-corpse-saturated self-portraits up to Odd Nerdrum's
paintings of classical agents dropped into tortured
psychogeographies—there is, more than ever today, an urgent
necessity to combine the ecstatic humanism of the OLD and
the devastating nihilism of the NOW through painting, against
painting, for painting! Certainly, I hear from some of the more
naïve undergraduates a call for art through revolution, art

against revolution, art for revolution! This must be avoided. It is tempting to relive the best days of the Gutai group or the Mono-ha or even try to rekindle the magic that was Futurism, Dada, and the Situationist International—but today's world is neither post-WWII japan nor turn-of-the-century Paris nor the Cabaret Voltaire Zurich nor May '68 Nanterre!!! Today is today! The social structures and media infrastructures to maintain individual isolation and loneliness are so much more concretised in the twenty-first century matrix. Simulation is not enough. What distinguishes us from the past is the quality of today's nihilism; its enormous speeds, its unprecedented ubiquity and ability to manœuvre, connive, survive—even as humanism attempts its endless peripheral counter-attacks. Utter ideological despair is not simply science fiction, it is an inevitability in today's New World Order. We hear the deafening screeching of the processions; we collapse to our knees, and wonder—what is to be done? I say paint. Forget relational aesthetics! Forget deskilled engagement!! Forget art for the everyday!!! We ought to bring about a new post-postmodernity and face the unmovable patchworked corpse that is postmodernity; without boring hesitation, without indignation and resentment, without superfluous hyperbole, without the lacklustre insecurities of today's ideologues, and surely without the nonsensical twentieth-century tools provided by the academy's absent-minded french theoreticians. There is a certain gap between philosophising and painting. And what we ought to learn to do over and over again, even if it takes us forever, is to heroically admit that there is a void, an unapproachable chasm, and there is nothing we can do as artists to bridge this gap. They say—deny it. I say—accept it. They say—engage it. I say—acknowledge it. They say—sit. I say—move. Kant got it right, this gap is the thing in itself!'

From Alice to Gertrude and back again

I was late for Maggie Nelson's seminar. Margaret is a poet, essayist and scholar with a PhD in english literature from the Graduate Center of the City University of New York. Her books include a mixed-genre narrative about the 1969 murder of her aunt Jane. Looks wise, she is a cross between artist Miri Segal and Tel Aviv Museum of Art curator Ellen Ginton. Red, light (sometimes blondish) hair. Green, maybe blue eyes depending on the light. We raced past the dirty white, cinder block drywall. Room A217. A heavy blue door. Disorientated anorexic dancers occupied the hall. Everything permeated with the smell of burnt popcorn and chalk.

We walked in to a dozen photogenic, artistically inclined faces. I recognised some of them. Burgess, the filmmaker. Heavy black-rimmed glasses. If I'd known I was going to write about him later, I'd have made some notes at the time. He was probably wearing a black jacket with a wicca insignia on the chest. And then there was the video artist Michelle Lee. Punk grrrl. I have not a clue what she was wearing. Short black hair. Piercing eyes. She reminded me of Janine. Michelle could've easily been a member of the japanese punk band, *Thug Murder*. Megan Collins, the photographer. John Gill, the Buddhist poet. Kiki Johnson, the historiographer. And then there was Leila. Startling brown or grey eyes. Leila's boyfriend with whom she'd have a son. Also present: Mister Romantic (Bradley) and Mister Misogynist (Dante). A green hat and a crab. A few others. Amra Brooks was sitting at the head of the table. She self-published her coming of age book, *California*. Brooks was this week's in-class guest.

Brooks criticised the notion of the memoir. She preferred to call *California* fiction. According to Brooks the 'memoir' implied a degree of wisdom and hindsight she felt uncomfortable claiming. Besides she didn't want to end up like James Frey. Today we read in the *Times* of Oprah's current book scandal! James Frey's memoir, *A Million Little Pieces*—replete with 'inconsistencies, exaggerations, or lies'. A similar problem with Norma Khouri's *Honor Lost*. And it turns out novelist JT Leroy is not really a transgendered, HIV-positive former prostitute but writer Laura Albert! Outrage! Ire!! Absolute indignation!!! Brooks found the public's reaction to all of this quite amusing. So did Janine. She had an intense laugh. Burgess asked Brooks how much of her novel was bullshit. Twenty per cent? Fifty per cent? Ninety per cent? She didn't offer a direct answer. She picked up a copy of her book. She had brought a stack to sell. Pink cover. A hand-drawn picture of a finch. The title of the book in capital-type; the type set was Times New Roman. Heroically DIY. I have the 2004 edition in front of me as I write. She signed it. *For ryu, Amra Brooks*. She had the same cursive style as Wanda Coleman.

4.25pm. Amra Brooks' many earrings and the ring. Right hand. Distracting. Margaret steered the conversation to myth making and the ethical importance of *facts*. I was immediately reminded of Walt Disney's cryogenically frozen head—somewhere in the sub-basement. Even Baudrillard had circulated this myth. Kathy Acker's frozen body—somewhere in the sub-sub-basement. Jeremy Bentham's head next to Disney's. Maggie explicated notions of 'autobiography as hoax' and the effervescent nature of 'history-making' to films by Andrei Tarkovsky and Jonathan Caouette's *Tarnation* (2003), movies we'd seen in her class. I suppose it's strange that I equate Tarkovsky's *The Mirror* (1974) as the cinematic equivalent to a Kathy Acker novel. Janine thinks it's because of the seemingly amorphous quality of both. Tarkovsky's 'arbitrary' use of flashbacks, historical footages and original poetry. Acker's 'arbitrary' use of high-canons and low-canons and EVERYTHING. The reader could pick up one of Kathy's books at any point. It was never necessary to read *Don Quixote* or *Pussy, King Of The Pirates* from cover to cover. I felt the same way about Tarkovsky's films. It was never necessary for me to view *Solaris* from beginning to end. The act of writing and reading and hearing and seeing is and ought to be a more spontaneous experience than the traditional novel/movie would have us believe. Of course, the same could not be said for Jonathan Caouette's film. It was heavily dependant on a traditional narrative scheme. The story of trauma: personal history making at its most manipulative. Dante: a false rape revenge narrative! Bradley: Psychosis!! Molly: Literal madness!!! It was all so contrived. Shameless. While Caouette's use of Super-8, video diaries, and early short films was admirable—all it amounted to was a lie. By the second viewing Janine hated it.

As the rest of the class shouted over each other, my mind began to act out. There is nothing inherently positive about discourse! There is nothing intrinsically good within the coordinates of cinema studies!! The emancipatory potential of literary criticism was quite low!!! These people had not watched Clark's video art, *10 Hours of Menstruation* (2006). But of course, here is the underlying paradox: no matter how much it stank, no matter how much it disappointed—I was entangled in the octopus tentacle mess. Discourse had dragged

me in without consent. Without permission. Without even
the courtesy of a reach around.

6.30pm. What is it to be narcissistic? Margaret had assigned us
to read Gertrude Stein's *The Autobiography of Alice B. Toklas*.
All those names. What is at the core of name-dropping? Is it
in part to convince the reader that she is indeed part of the in-
crowd? Henry James. Pablo Picasso. Ernest Hemingway.
Stieglitz. Matisse. Maddening. The list goes on and on (and the
beat don't stop till the break of dawn). Are we convinced she
is in the proper literary/art circles? She is a narcissist. Stein's
ability to speak in Alice's voice (a voice not of her own, a voice
tacitly given). Is it not the case that really Stein is just using the
literary opportunity to talk about herself? Maggie disagrees.
Maxi disagrees. Gina disagrees. According to one of Gina
Clark's emails: 'oh, narcicism… damn, i can never spell that
right. i think what i was trying to at, was that love is mainly
dangerous becuse we often look for our own qualities in
another person, because were mostly fascinated with our selves,
our own mind, our own habits and functions. its difficult not to
be… (fascinated with the personal self). We can only encounter
"ourselves" or our bodies through reflections, whether it be
video, photographs, audio, etc… I feel that narcicism, isnt such
a terrible thing, more like a natural and even more animalistic
sensation that is ever present. we will never know ourselves
outside of our view from the top of our shoulders… its kind
of depressing. goes back to my obsession with nostalgic
sensations. its memory, how we learn and develop, as the
animals which we are.'

According to Maxi it's often been said by the likes of Ammiel
Alcalay and Sesshu Foster and Jane Sprague (members
decidedly in the non-normative camp) that american texts are
all too often—too 'solitary' and too 'alone' (in other words we

have no 'collective memory'). From this vantage point it is clear why Gertrude Stein would want to 'use' Alice (you see, the poet doesn't want to be so normatively 'solitary' and 'alone') to gain a kind of radical identity, an identity not limited by 'I' or 'e'—but refocused and in the process reconnected with other artists (building a kind of mini-community through the W[I]e or the 'weee'). Maxi would argue this is the way that Alice contests the dominant 'normative narrative' that rewards heterosexual 'solitude', maleness, and anglo-saxonism in general. As a weapon, a kind of grenade or ammunition for the mini-Steins of the world, *The Autobiography of Alice B. Toklas* is an effective tool at disarming the enemy.

But then again, what about the irritation and the kind of Sartrean nausea one feels after reading one of Stein's para-prose pieces? Or after reading one of Steve Erickson's novels? I can certainly see the Anti-Sesshu Fosters and the Anti-Jane Spragues of the world point to Steinian irritation as a reason not to join the anti-regime, but to excitedly and with vigour hold up the banner of classical humanism. Certainly, students of Harold Bloom have made such arguments. In fact many have labelled Stein as part of the 'Chaotic Age,' an age of disrepair and general dumbness that came after the 'Democratic Age'. Both arguments are tactically sound when given their full vigor and context. Let us now move on to Roland Barthes. Its very strangeness and the fact that Barthes was 'gay' and that his supposed autobiography isn't one, is more than enough for the *nons* to conceivably 'use' Barthes as one of their own. His heavy dependence on theory, *cruising*, and method broadens autobiography, broadens (or destroys, depending on your regime) what it means to be an intellectual, an artist. But of course, we also find it irritating and the juxtapositioning of disparate elements often befuddles. Enter the faux Blooms of the world. You see!? You see how nonsensical french theory is!?

We only have so many books to read (ironically the same argument that Alcalay uses)—let us resort to the canons, let us drop Stein and Barthes and pick up Shakespeare and Dante!!! Long live the canon!! And death to the philistines and plebs that seek to burn GOOD books!

After Maggie's class, Janine and I went to Kyoto Sushi (a mediocre-korean owned restaurant, five minutes away from the Institute) and ate rainbow rolls with tempura dishes. The fake sushi was horrible. They had even managed to screw up the tempura. Janine drank an imported nigori sake, I drank a glass of Kirin. Janine asked me how many people I knew in Santa Clarita. I asked Janine how many people she knew in the city. Not many. She'd been living in Tokyo for the last two summers. Her relationship with her biological father was a complicated one. What a coincidence. I was leaving for Tokyo in four days. Why had she come back to the states? Apparently, a Professor _____ had urged her to get her master's at CalArts. The anglophantic faculty at The University of Tokyo endlessly circulated the factoid that The Institute is indeed the first higher educational institute in the states to offer undergraduate and graduate degrees in both visual and performing arts. Janine asked why I was leaving for japan. I told her it was complicated. The conversation somehow got to Kathy Acker. *Are you close with Matias?* I nodded yes. This was of course a lie. I knew him as well as I knew Johnny, the first of the sacred seven. I hardly knew the literary executor. *How did you two meet?*

Tokyo, japan is exciting and peaceful. I was young when I was first asked to teach in Tokyo and talked japanese there and was photographed there and went to school there, and ate miso soup for early breakfast and had sashimi and spinach for lunch, I always like spinach, and a black cat jumped on the

Chancellor's back. That was more exciting than peaceful. I do not mind cats but I do not like them to jump on my back. There are lots of cats in Tokyo and in japan and they can do what they like, stay in or go out. It is extraordinary that they fight so little among themselves considering how many cats there are. There are two things that japanese animals do not do, cats do not fight much and do not howl much and dogs do not get flustered running across the road, if they start to cross the road they keep on going which is what japanese and english people do too.

Kato's party was hosted by one of his publisher friends. Back then he was not the physical specimen he is now. I didn't know it at the time but Kato had bailed out Kondansha International on more than one occasion (with quick selling University Press titles such as *Kogals: Japan's Urban Teenage Girl Culture* and *Subcultured: 90s Japanese Punk Rock and Beyond).* The new apartment was on the tenth floor of the Miyoshi, one of the closest to the university. You'd never seen anything like it. A dramatic balcony. Books everywhere in the spacious living room. Indian rugs. A working kotatsu. Bookcases, even in the two bathrooms. A cute kitchen—chrome, cherry tea towels, white tiles. Fun! Pink granite island. The bedrooms were separated with walls constructed out of translucent steel beams (unheard of outside of Tokyo) and transparent green glass. It successfully created the illusion of depth. It is a self-consciously postmodern piece of architectural design. Not my wet dream.

The guest list was amazing. Can you believe it? Takashi Miike, the notoriously prolific director auteur (and his entourage, mainly fashion designers and surfers). Jung-neem Kim, the mother of two prominent korean economists. Dr. Takashi Murakami, otaku artist and founder of the Superflat movement (and his entourage, essentially young artists). Ryu Murakami, the 'enfant terrible' of japanese literature (and his entourage, mainly politicos and hip nihilists). John Gill, Buddhist scholar and co-founder of Neo-Annihilism, Stuffism, Sprawl, and Euboop. Yoshimi, musician. Athena Lynn, political theatrician. The Methamphibian duo, the Los-Angeles based shoe customisers. The girls of *Thug Murder*, a japanese oi-slash-punk band (Ryoko Naito—Guitar and vocals. Chisato Otsubo—Bass. Yurie Sakuma—Drums). SABU, director. Fukawa, the sculptor. Kim Ki-duk, the korean filmmaker. Jen Hofer, poet and editor and translator of *Sin Puertas Visibles*. Jacquelyn Davis, poet and founder of *valeveil*. Matt Timmons, sound poet. Ara Shirinyan, transcoded text poet. Peter Chung, creator of *Aeon Flux*. Matias Viegener, the literary executor of Kathy Acker and editor and co-translator of Georges Bataille's *The Trial of Gilles de Rais*.

The first time I spoke to him, Matias was sitting alone on the balcony. Cross-legged. A cigarette in one hand and a glass of ji-biru in the other. I could swear I'd seen him before. I mean not at the party or in japan, but back in the states. He was wearing a black, collared shirt. Black jeans. A pair of Nike's in retro Milwaukee Bucks colours. I instantly found him of interest. For whatever reason his face reminded me of Joaquin Phoenix's or a young Johnny Cash. I approached him. He awoke. I could tell the party meant very little to him; he was too immersed, too intoxicated in the skyline. Hiragana graphics, moving colours, neon billboards, and of course Fuji-san, billowing, extending, propping up the night sky. He sat up. Brown eyes. I saw sadness in them, a profound but familiar sadness. He was obviously somewhere else and I felt guilty for disturbing him.

'Hello.'
'Konnichiwa.'
'Excuse me?'

'Kon-ni-chi-wa.'

'Konnichiwa?'

'Kon-NI-chhhiii-wa.'

'Hai.'

'Gomennasai.'

'Sumimasen.'

'Watashiwa nihongowo amari umaku hanasemasen.'

'Mousukoshi yukkuri hanashite kudasai.'

'Wa-ta-ssshhhhhhiii-wa niiii-hon-goooo-wooo a-maaaari u-maaaa-ku haaaa-na-se-maaaaa-sen.'

'Mouchido ittekudasai.'

'Waaaaa-taaaa-ssshhhhhhiiiiii-wa niiiii-hooooon-gooooooo-woooooo aaaaaa-maaaaa-riiiiii uuuuuuuuuuuuuuuuuuuuuuuuuu-maaaaaaaaaaaaa-kuuuuuuuuuuu haaaaaaaaaaaaa-naaaaaaaaaaa-sssseeeeeeeeeeeeeeee-maaaaaaaaaa-seeeeeeeeeeeeeeeeen.'

'Mougamandekinai!'

'Choushiwadou?'

'Genkidesu.'

'Onamaewa?'

'Watashino namaewa Ryu desu. Onamaewa?'

'Matias.'

'Matias, your japanese is very good. I'm sorry. Did you want to be alone?' I asked.

'No, no. Just a little drunk. Please, have a seat.' Matias turned to look past the floor to ceiling glass doors. 'So how's the party?'

'Um – good, I guess. Miike's a lot of fun.' Matias nodded in agreement.

'Can I bum a cigarette off you?' I asked.

'Actually, this is my last one. But here, have it.'

'No, that's fine.'

'Please, go ahead. I smoke too much anyway.' I took the cigarette from his fingers and took a quick drag. The wind

picked up. Exhaled. I gave back the smoke. We admired
the view.

'My real name's Maxi by the way.'

'Matias.'

'So what are you doing here?'

'You mean in japan or just in general?'

'In japan.'

'Well,' he took a quick drag, 'several things actually. Visiting
friends — most of whom don't speak japanese. Trying to relax.
Oh, I highly recommend the hot springs in Matsuyama if you
haven't been. And um, really just, kind of struggling to work on
my book about Kathy.'

I smiled and took a sip of my Ise beer. 'So you're a novelist?'

'Well, with a host of others I look after Kathy Acker. I also
teach at Cal Art.'

'So that's where I remember you from. I knew I've seen you
before.' I was excited.

'Did you go to Cal Art?'

'No, but my friend did. Miju (a different Miju).'

'Sure. I remember her. Mohawk. Evil eye.'

I laughed, I put my bottle down. 'Actually, this is my last day
in japan. I'm meeting her or I'm supposed to meet her in Jeju
Island tomorrow. My flight leaves at eight.'

'How is she doing?'

'Better. Much better.' He took a sip of his beer. I took a sip of
mine. He understood what I was referring to. Uncomfortable
silence.

'Have you ever been to Jeju before?' he asked.

'No.'

'You're going to love it,' Matias assured me. 'Much prettier
than Hawaii. Gorgeous volcano. Lovely people.' He handed me
the cigarette. The music in the living room turned from japanese
ambient electronica to a shonen-knife cover. Lots of laughter.
I turned to look past the glass.

'So Max, what do you do?'

'Trying to write. Working on a book.'

'Really?'

'Yes. It takes place mostly in japan and The Institute.'

'Have you started sending it out?'

'Actually, Canonbait's interested.'

'No kidding?' half-shocked.

I confessed to him that I was equally surprised by Canonbait's letter. I explained to him I'd always associated the independent publishing house with plagiarism and Mister Trippy's brand of anarchism. But according to Matias—ever since October, when they became independent again following a management buy-out, the Edinburgh-based publishing house re-emerged with the goal of having a distinctly international outlook. Really just another way of funnelling new revenues. Hence the Ferguson titles. They had no qualms about exploiting the niche market. *What genre?* I told him my novel was science fiction and we talked about Philip K. Dick. I was born in the same year he died. Never got to see the final version of 'Blade Runner' (a film that keenly exploited the japanese psychogeography). Matias didn't know he was a gnostic. *Did you know he believed that time didn't exist—that really it's no more 2006 than it is 20 BC?* Time is an illusion created by the anti-christ, (or to you, dear reader and me) anti-literary demons, the Evils of the world to make everyone think that they're not in eternity, that you're not in god's or the canon's everlasting presence and grace and love and minor thoughts. By accepting the past, present, and future—we say no to god (or in Žižek's case—'Death Drive'). Constantly no to transcendence. But to say yes. Yes to the infinite—really all you have to do is say yes to the moment. Because the moment is infinite. You see? All one has to recognise is that the time is now. Not then, but NOW. Not now, but *now*. *NOW*. *Now*. Now.

After we finished the saki I suggested we go back to The Institute. 8pm was when David Earle and Maxi Kim would give thesis presentations at Butler Building 4. Many of the prospective students would be attending. Because we were drunk we decided to walk. Although CalArts was a cultural oasis, the surrounding Valencia town centre was a pedestrianised shopping nightmare. Disgust was written all over Janine's face. By the time we got to Butler Building 4 the thesis presentations were half over. We caught the tale end of the raucous polemic by Dante West, the resident anti-hero: '*Seek not the plebeians—for they too sodomise stinking corpses! Beware the Philistine—for she too will dig up the dead! Trust not the proletariat—they too own shovels! Distrust the capitalist—for he owns guns! And never, ever—whatever your cause—hand your trust blindly over to an academic; for HE will not only rape the dead, but rape the living. HE'll drag your half-dead body up to a red hill and there—he will take his fuck stick and jam it in to your mind. Rolling it back and forth on your cerebrum, he will force you to take one of his balls in your mouth and nip playfully at the sack that contains them. A few minutes later it won't be hard to get him to come in your mouth. So beware. You are you. They are them. What's at stake here are your dreams, your identity, your life. Not theirs. Ask yourself— WHAT DO I TRULY DESIRE? HOW DID I BECOME MYSELF?*'

The room was packed. I suggested we go to The Cube instead, the space directly adjacent to 4. We walked in to an intellectual cock-fight. M. Cantsin and Karen Eliot and Burgess and Michelle (I've overheard them screwing in the basement darkrooms) were talking over each other. A bottle of beaulieu cabernet was opened along with two bottles of pinot. Janine and I helped ourselves to the cabernet. The source of all the distress? As Michelle explained it to me Karen solicited Burgess' opinion

on the whole Oprah book scandal. Burgess found the public's
reaction to James Frey's memoir quite amusing. So did Max.
To expect precise, journalistic truth from literature was utterly
absurd. The height of absurdity, Burgess exclaimed! One must
allow the writer a degree of artistic license. To exaggerate,
embellish certain aspects of life. As Nietzsche proclaimed
there're kernels of truths even in hyperboles. Even in lies. Even
in untruths. Max being Burgess' friend chimed in with a few of
his own observations. Readers ought to have an understanding
of the para-fictional (Max learned that word from Jon Wagner).
Can you imagine readers being offended by Leonid Tsypkin's
Summer In Baden-Baden (even though he never knew
Dostoyevsky personally? Shocking!)? Or Banti's *Artemisia*
(witchcraft!) or Elizabeth Hardwick's *Sleepless Nights*. Do we
really care if there actually was a little boy in a nursery school
(40)? If we discovered it was not 'a small yellow ball, a ball of
the purest yellow like the colour of the early forsythia then
coming into bloom in Central Park' but a small pink ball, a
ball of the dirtiest pink like the colour of a wilting Zépherine
Drouhin—would we really care? As para-readers we are willing
to relinquish to the artist a degree of artistic license, freedom.
After all, aren't all books lies? Even memoirs? Even non-fiction
books? Structuring a book, even structuring your 'distorted
memories' (as Hardwick understands it) is a lie. But of course,
the philistine can not have this. Especially, when the lyric is at
play. How dare our Elizabeth juxtaposition such flowery
descriptions (e.g. 23) to tug at our heartstrings! To manipulate
us in order 'to feel'. To think. But as Sesshu Foster reminds us
— 'Movies do that all the time'. Sensing that Burgess and Max
were being unfair, the boys' club ganging up on Karen, Michelle
offered up her own observations.

After a while Karen Eliot and M. Cantsin had had enough.
We heard the thesis presentations end with a roar of applause.

Faculty members, old MFA students, prospective MFA students flooded in to The Cube for the wine and beer and cheese. The Red Lioness was wearing what can only be described as an artisanal chocolate bar wrapper crinkled and wound by an obsessive-compulsive. This was Matias' description. I envied women. australian/ british women. They could wear extravagant hats without being self-conscious. The Red Lioness was speaking with Matias. She is a trained critical thinker with a doctorate in philosophy and literature, and a background in studio arts. Her favourite novel is *Moby Dick*. Janine went to introduce herself. I was drowsy with sleep. Michelle and Burgess were still arguing. Philistine! Nazi! Too much alcohol. That night I dreamt I was the Red Lioness.

Bretonites, Dadaists, Surrealists rejoice! For dream time is upon us!!!

This is the story of Christine and Margaret (both born from the same womb, raised in the same room, disciplined with the same broom). How does one come to love the gratuitous precision of tautological syllogisms (i.e. the Red Lioness is australian, and all australians are human, and therefore the Red Lioness is a human being)? In the narrow prefecture of Tokyo-to, there once lived a member of the bourgeoisie; an unusually attractive, very pretentious, exceedingly wealthy australian girl by the name of Christine. I detested her. I will not go in to all of the reasons why (because this round-about exegesis has to be about her feelings, not mine) but I will admit—there's been countless times when I've fantasised about tearing her flesh from her ample breasts and buttocks with red-hot pincers. Afterwards, I am outside my body (the body of the text) and I see myself pouring burning resin where the flesh was torn away. *EEEEEEEEEEEE!!!* I'd listen intently to her cries and moans. Because she was educated, she was not accustomed to such treatment. My self-assigned task was to re-educate her. Because she was a person of privilege, she was content to believe she was somehow a 'literal' manifestation of power. Let us disabuse her of such academically bourgeois notions by using our implementations of power (e.g. a red-hot pincer to her pale face and a disciplinary apparatus to the posterior opening).

Christine and her sister loved each other. In Tokyo they lived comfortably, enjoying the twenty-four hour amenities, attending art museums, taking advantage of the interdisciplinary networks at the university. I, on the other hand, detested Tokyo. All the automobile exhaust and cedar pollen was physically aggravating. The lack of trees, gardens, and overall green spaces appalled me. And Tokyo's so-called investments in traditional japanese arts were laughable. I'd have lived in Kyoto, had I not been attending the university. One day, the two of them (after several minutes of foreplay and eventual coitus) plotted to murder their (M)other. I know this because I live in the apartment next to theirs and the walls are thin. As for their reasons for wanting to slaughter glamorous academicians like their (M)other—I could not understand their arguments. But if my memory is to be trusted, the conversation was based on capricious economic—slash—literary models.

Christine: We should start with our (M)other.

Maggie: But I thought you liked her comforting baths.

Christine: For a good fuck—boy are you dense. It isn't about whether or not I liked her class. That shouldn't be the criteria one uses to decide whether or not to take another person's life.

Margaret: Explain it to me again.

Christine: According to the Decadent Action Manifesto (as printed in page one of *Mind Invaders: A Reader In Psychic Warfare, Cultural Sabotage And Semiotic Terrorism / Edited By Mister Trippy)*—'Decadent Action are a High Street anarchist guerrilla organisation whose main aim is to destroy the capitalist system by a leisurely campaign of good living and overspending. We plan to achieve our aims by making capitalism fall on its own sword. If you neglect and ignore capitalism it will not go away, but feed it to excess for long enough and it will eventually burst. /We use the simple economic principles of supply and demand with their intrinsic link to inflation to establish the correctness of our theories. The state must control these factors to run the economy efficiently; throw in the wild card of massive irrational overspending on seemingly random luxury goods and the government is unable to take control. This will lead to hyperinflation and large-scale social unrest, in turn leading to the collapse of the monetary system and disintegration of the state apparatus. /So how can you get involved in this conspiracy to overthrow the government without making too much effort or getting your hands dirty? Well, the answer is to spend, spend, spend! Get money, spend it; it's as simple as that'.

Margaret: But Chris, what the fuck does any of that have to do with killing our (M)other?

Christine: Shut up! I'm getting to that. Obviously, the above diatribe isn't supposed to be taken wholly seriously. Obviously, overspending isn't going to lead to large-scale social unrest. If that was the case 'To-o-kyo-o' wouldn't be home to 12.7 million people. But even with all of its erroneous intellectual leaps, Decadent Action is right on one point. Something has to be done about japan's current cultural clime. Obviously, we can't take on the state. We are neither large enough nor enthused enough to take on such a Goliath. However, we—being two bourgeois, unusually attractive, very pretentious, exceedingly wealthy australian sisters—have free access to a cultural institution very dear and near to our hearts. The University. A glamorous intellectual such as our (M)other is part of that institution and is in the way of cultural progress. She peddles western 'canons' and their offsprings (i.e. William Shakespeare, James Joyce, William Faulkner, Ernest Hemingway) as if western 'canons' were somehow separate from nature, concurrently acting as anti-dialectical inversions propagated by OLD WHITE SAINTS! What we need to do now is return to a truly nippon-centric literary revolution where writers such as Shinzaburo Iketani, Nobuko Yoshiya, Chiyo Uno, Kokuseki Oizumi, Kansuke Naka, Kiku Amino, Ken (Takeru) Inukai, Kosaku Takii, Yuriko Chujo, Shiro Ozaki, Chiaki Shimomura—reignite the psychogeographical landscape. Killing our (M)other is the first step, and it's a small price to pay considering the millions of future cultural-nomads that will benefit from our actions today.

That night I couldn't get Christine's words out of my head, and as a result I dreamt I was her. I/she dreamt I/she was ascending a metaphor. You didn't always want to burn books. There was a time before you became well-acquainted with the Red Lioness, before you had to commute to Tokyo, before you got accepted into your mother's university when the thought of dousing paperbacks in gasoline and then igniting it—never would've even crossed your mind—let alone fill you with such

sexual pleasure and adrenaline (as it did right now). Yet here
you were, your panties wet, on top of holy Fuji-san with the
Red Lioness standing on the peak of a pile of overdue library
books. You don't ask how she ever managed to lug them all—all
the way to the top of Mt. Fuji. She must've befriended graduate
students. H. Abramowitz. H. Bursch. *Gina Clark*. K. English.
B. Folkerts. K. Johnson. Allison Carter. H. Clawford. J. David.
Duke Earle. D. Fever. C. Garfield. Beth Randall. M. McDuffy.
L. Nicholas. Jared Olsen. Michaele Simmer. Nadine Rambo.
D. Ruiz. Danielle Adair. E. Ekland. Joseph Pottsville.
S. Finnerky. J. Hall. L. Venal. S. Wangstein. A. Lambertstein.
Romantic Powells. A.M. Jitters. Cat Wolfstein. Uncle Joe.
Beatles McCartney. R. Yourick. Nick Gritzer. Kian Park.
K. Catchall. Erik Landline. Stephan Van Dyck. A. El
Bahirowitz. S.M. Archipellego. There must be at least a
thousand paperbacks. You note the names that are about to
be cremated. They are names you are vaguely familiar with.

Jane Austen. Sylvia Plath. Ayn Rand. Charlotte Brontë. Emily
Brontë. Kathy Acker. Anne Sexton. Pauline Réage. Mar…
but wait. Oh no. It can't be. You begin now to understand the
logical fallacy behind your/her own syllogism. If Christine
thinks that all white writers are culturally destructive within a
japanese paradigm and all culturally destructive claims must be
destroyed, then even white, female writers (which she admires
greatly) would have to be barred. Yes, you see the scheme
unraveling quickly. First, The (M)other. Then Professor J.
Wagner. Then S. Erickson. B. Mullens. J. Sarbane. B. Bauman.
When would it end? You understand now that what she really
wants is not a cultural renovation, a cultural revolution—but
cultural anarchy. And she's using the dumb M and her 'pseudo-
socialist' leanings to a horrific end. She's clever. But how will I
stop her? I'm going to stop her. I'll confront her and I'll use the
gratuitous precision of her tautological syllogisms against her.

The following evening. Promptly at seven o'clock. I arrived
at her apartment door. I knew I wouldn't win her over
ideologically with simple anti-anarchic rhetoric so I brought
along some spicy tuna and a few cans of jizake, a 'regional sake'
brand (equivalent to german kolsch in american
microbreweries). As expected she opened the door wearing
her Ramones wifebeater. There was no trace of Margaret except
her jissom. Her apartment surprised me in that it was exactly
the way I pictured it. There was no furniture. Only some used
condoms on the floor along with several tall bookcases full of
'anti-canons'. I recognised some of the names. Sakujiro Kano.
Taizo Soma. A spunk-stained Jun Tanaka. Zenzo Kasai. Koji
Uno. Yi In-jik. Yi Hae-cho. Ch'oe Ch'an-shik. Kim
(pronounced cheme as in scheme) Ko-je. Seiji Tanizaki. Kazuo
Hirotsu. A bloodstained Jane Austen. Sylvia Plath. Ayn Rand.
Charlotte Brontë. Kathy Acker. Anne Sexton. Pauline Réage.
Mary Oliver. Yuzo Yamamoto. Musoan Takebayashi. Saisei
Muro. Seikichi Fujimori. A bloodstained Kiyosshi Eguchi.
Hyakken Uchida. Kichiji Nakatogawa. Mosaku Sasaki.
Masajiro Kojima. Kyota Mizuki. Haruo Sato. A bloodstained
Yuzuru Matsuoka. Masao Kume. Yoshio Tokyoshima. Kan
Kikuchi. Ryunosuke Akutagawa. Michel Foucault's *Discipline
and Punish*.

As we sat, I got her loaded and we both shared the spicy tuna.
She commented on the fact that the sushis were the Miyamoto
special recipe variety. I complimented her on her sensitive
palate. She complimented me on my fine selection of alcohol.
Not a lot of people understand japanese microbreweries and
my penchant for saki bordered on the elitist. As we began to
talk about what I overheard the other night, she quickly
disabused me of any murderous plots or crazy cultural
revolution schemes. Apparently, she and her sister got really
blitzed after they had just gotten out of Ryu's lecture. What I

had heard was sophomoric rantings fuelled by Suntory (most likely) and the post-feminist illuminations of a riot grrrl. I was relieved. I told her about my dream. She was sympathetic. She brought out some rainbow kiwifruit roll and I admired the way she presented the wasabi and pickled ginger. As I ate she began to tell me about a similar dream she had a few days ago. In it she played the metaphorical role of Princess Amaradevi in the famous South-East Asian oral-tale, *The Story of Princess Amaradevi*. I was intrigued by the psychological parallels and I had to empty my bladder. I asked her where the toilet was.

As I relieved myself my unrelenting hatred for Christine quickly evaporated. It turned out she wasn't the bourgeois, unusually attractive, very pretentious, exceedingly wealthy australian girl I had made her out to be. Although, some of her biblio-tastes were indicative of a bourgeois mind set, much of her library was that of a reader invested in early-twentieth-century nippon—slash—korean literature. And from the absence of any furniture in her bleak apartment, it was clear that the rent was being financed by her parents. They were probably middle-class. She had probably told them the apartment was self-furnished to save them the extra cost. Considerate Christine. Clever Margaret.

As I zipped up and was about to flush, something struck me as odd. The fog of her intoxicating female essence had cleared. The well-structured narrative made no sense at all. It didn't stand to reason. If her parents were wealthy enough to buy her shelf after shelf of expensive books, they were surely rich enough to buy her a few sticks of furniture. Had she sold the proppings? Thrown them out? Why? And the bloodstained copies of Austen and Eguchi and Matsuoka. And then suddenly the mental dam broke, followed by a flood of horrific possibilities. Perhaps they had brought the (M)other's fresh corpse in to the apartment and she had bled. Perhaps they had drugged the woman and then butchered her at home. Oh no, the copy of *Discipline and Punish*. Had they tortured her? Tortured her as I was going to torture Christine? Inconceivable. Calm down. Breathe. You're getting ahead of yourself. Calm down. You sit down on the ledge of the bath and push the shower curtain to the side. The (M)other's tortured body. Your stomach turns. You recoil at first, but you don't run out of the bathroom. Maintain composure! The grey-cells in your cerebrum fire and misfire at an exceedingly dangerous clip and the syllogism you wanted to use to convince the girl barrels out of your mouth.

ALL AUSTRALIANS ARE HUMANISTS. HUMANISTS CAN'T KILL HUMAN BEINGS. THE RED LIONESS IS AUSTRALIAN, AND THEREFORE A HUMAN BEING. CHRISTINE IS AUSTRALIAN. CHRISTINE IS A HUMANIST. CHRISTINE CAN'T KILL HUMAN BEINGS. CHRISTINE CAN'T KILL THE (M)OTHER. But then you realise. Christine. Chris-tine. That isn't an australian accent at all. Of course, she was english. The horrible sight of the (M)other's severed sinews. According to Foucault 'the infinitesimal destruction of the body is linked here with spectacle: each piece is placed on display. /The execution was accompanied by a whole ceremonial of triumph; but it also included, as a dramatic nucleus in its monotonous progress, a scene of confrontation: this was the immediate, direct action of the executioner on the body of the "patient". It was a coded action, of course, since custom and, often quite explicitly, the sentence prescribed its principal episodes. Nevertheless, it did preserve something of the battle'.

And I am reminded of Mister Trippy's *Mind Invaders*. 'The days of this society are numbered. Its reasons and its merits have been weighed in the balance and found wanting; its inhabitants are divided into two parties, one of which wants to build their own… and leave this society behind… Dream time is upon us…'

Find y'r inner Tiger Shark, Jon said

I was born in Tarzana, California. I have in consequence always preferred living in a windy climate but it is difficult, on the continent of East Asia or even in america, to find a windy climate and live in it. Before M___ was M___ he was Ryu. And before that he was an I. And if you subscribe to the vision of my Buddhist friend, John Gill – all of time is a merry-go-round. Historical genesis as farce! WEEEEEEEEEEEEEE!!! After much pushing and laughing, it is conceivable to say that after M is Janine he is Miju. And after that he becomes an I. Here's a theory: all young writers, emerging artists start out with the I out of a deep sense of panic, frustration and desperation. *To be somebody. Is this not the fatal flaw?* One takes on all kinds of prejudices in the name of artistry. But of course, as with anything, the fear evaporates and all that is left is a general ____ of nothingness. This objectivity or cretin clarity if you want, is a gift. Possibly the greatest of gifts from the omniverse. This is an increasingly familiar adventure! It certainly is M___.

8:30 am. April 23. I was sleepy. It was an overcast, spring morning. Main parking lot. 'You're late. You're seeking.' 'Seeking what?' 'You're seeking attention.' 'I'm sorry — I'm just really lost today.' 'You're always lost.' 'I don't know. Particularly lost today. Bad karma.' 'Get the load in the car.' I misheard. 'And what are we disposing of today? What prehistoric delight invites our unfortunate gaze?' M___ had experienced serious doubts about Harold Bloom in the past.

He also had unfavourable opinions about Cornel West and a few side salads. Dalai Lama and Habermas, I think. What he wanted to do was totally cleanse society from humanism. His idea was that it was too stupid. Too naïve. And that humanism today was a cover for something much more insidious. Ryu found great comfort in simulation. He found no comfort in the real. For him reality was a total obscenity. He found no meaning in it. darfur. The tsunami. Holocaust. Gulags. Re-education camps. Too many corpses. For the divided peninsula too (M___'s homeland) the twentieth century was a devastatingly obscene nightmare.

Why was Ryu interested in (M)iju? Why was he so enchanted with the Other? Perhaps because he saw in her a kind of simulation. Since forever, Ryu's been both softened and hardened by books such as Sylvia Plath's *The Bell Jar* and J.D. Salinger's *Franny and Zooey*. And more recently Banana Yoshimoto's *Goodbye Tsugumi*. Michelle Tea's *The Passionate Mistakes And Intricate Corruption Of One Girl In America*. Bernadette Corporation's *Reena Spaulings*. Louise Rennison's *On The Bright Side, I'm Now The Girlfriend Of A Sex God*. And Chun Sue's *Beijing Doll*. What all of these books had in common was the rape-revenge narrative. Whenever Miju asked him what the term meant— Ryu would hem and haw, not define it. (w)EEEEEEEEEEEEEEE!!! Maybe he didn't know. Or more likely it was an open-ended term like Art. No need to overdefine, lose sleep over it. All the books were tainted with the cumming-of-age aura; the art of the white foam was always nihilistic for Ryu—but it always contained within it the murky promise of hope. *Hope that wasn't difficult to eviscerate.* *EEEEEEEEEEEEEEEEEEEEEEEEEEEEEEEE!*

Of course, M___ had many gaps in his line of reasoning. We trudged through the trash. Much of what he talked about had that coy iconoclasm of that hack, white haired turkey. You could intuit the explicit gaps in the tangle of burnt-out fantasies and broken dreams. But to his credit, he understood that there was nothing intrinsically positive to KNOWL(E)DGE—that is to say, really (E)V(e)RYTHING depended on circumstance. This or that. This was radically contingent on that. O taking out his eye because he had the knowledge of fucking his mum and killing his pops—this is no good. *Which artist ought I imitate?* Of course, it isn't as simple as all that. To be much more precise: *which artist ought I incorporate, modify, hybridise?* So the journey is complicated by the fact that you yourself conscientiously desire to be part of a taut-linear tradition; but nonetheless, simultaneously separate from, uniquely shiny and autonomous. A more intellectual Andy Warhol? A more abject Cindy Sherman? A more dynamic Agnes Martin? A less frenetic Jackson Pollock? A more new age Damien Hirst? A more *japanese* Takashi Murakami? A more *korean* Nam June Paik? A more narrative-driven Bill Viola? A less repetitive Amy Adler? A more articulate Malerie Marder? A less punky Raymond Pettibon? A less ironic Barbara Kruger? A more subversive, politically explicit Thomas Hirschhorn? A more pre-modern Matthew Barney? A more bell hooks-inspired Kara Walker? A non-round, non-circular, less humanistic Atsuko Tanaka? A more commercial, post-fluxus inspired Ray Johnson? A more theory-driven, less conceptually-driven Jack Goldstein? A more deliberate, feminist-minded Jenny Holzer? The gap in between or '_____!' is an enigmatic one; it represents that grand canyon-gulf between what an artist actually is in his or her miserable, stupid reality and what he or she secretly, desperately desires to become—*only in dreams.*

—Ryu: glass shards, bits of rope, copies of Hokusai's 36 Views of Mt Fuji—although all rendered with a keen eye for aesthetics, good form, sincere energy—what exactly is the

point? Ryu, you ARE talented—no doubt about that—
but you have to have something more to say, something
alongside—it can't just BE process. FIND INNER TIGER
SHARK! Let's meet for tea tomorrow at my office 1:30 x Jon.

There is nothing quite as traumatic as that first set of
penultimate recommendations, a dashed scribble, the carefully-
worded notes. But thankfully for Ryu it was his second year
and he'd gone through a whole battery of critique sessions (and
the thinly veiled insults and traumatic innuendos that went with
them). Already a glaze began to develop; a buffer for his fragile
ego. Like immortal Miju, Ryu was a young visual arts student
with tremendous aspirations; he had gotten used to Wagner's
lukewarm responses, but a part of him still desired his mentor's
unremitting approval. *FIND INNER TIGER SHARK!*
He couldn't account for it; what had he done wrong? He'd
known that his mentor often praised the works of Amy Adler;
imitation, simulation, appropriation, plagiarism, repetition.
Was this not the mantra of the post-art, anti-everything era?
This is what he had done with the Hokusai prints. To inject
a bit of Jasper Johns' humour in to the dead corpse of a great
japanese master. If only he'd subscribed to *ARTFORUM*, he
would've known better. He would've gotten a better reception
if only he'd insinuated a bit of that glib Damien Hirst energy
in to chinese canons. More than anything else he wants to
produce meaning out of this world. This chaos. This shit-rock.
But it is difficult for Miju. She sat on the cold steps looked
down at the stairs below, past the black metal gates—and saw
something too elevated, too dangerous, the impossibility of this
world. The ridiculous laughter. Downstairs sparse piano music.
Upstairs eighties rock and roll. Why is it that Miju can only be
a schizophrenic? Was this something CalArts had done to her?
Made her strange, sick, nihilistic? Could it be that CalArts was
a cancer on her soul, her unceremonious jouissance, and her

will to becoming, becomed, etc? Why is the world about to turn upside down and drown itself? Why couldn't bad things stop happening? Or why couldn't bad things happen only to bad people? Obviously, many gaps here — like, who would decide who was good and who was bad? *The auteur?* Was there anything intrinsic to the numbness, the nothingness that she felt as he witnessed the trauma? Was there anything intrinsically more meaningful about what she felt NOW? Was there anything intrinsic in how he felt about her yesterday? And how he felt about her at this very moment? If it's all just relative — *I can think whatever the fuck I want to think*. So feel good, he thought. Only exist for your art. Why? Why not? Amy Adler was a seemingly successful artist; her 2001 project, *Amy Adler Photographs Leonardo DiCaprio* at the Photographers Gallery in London was her breakthrough hit. Ryu wanted so desperately to hold on to Issa's vile maxim. It went something like this: *To a prospective student: Don't imitate me. It's as boring as cutting two halves of a melon.*

I don't remember when I woke up or where I met Jon Wagner. I found myself in his office, the one above the Super Shop. It is a stunning black and red six-storey building that overlooks the music hall, the ostentatious Disney Lecture Hall and the length and width of the campus. I've always thought of it as an imposing structure with its translucent walls made out of red glass and a dramatic slant from the east wall to the west. From within one could admire the distant Santa Susannas to the west. On top of the slanting roof is a green house exclusively made for Jon's terrifying orchids, his own hybrids. Wagner's office is on the fifth floor right below the orchid garden. The first time I entered his room I was pleasantly surprised by the number of books, all of them related in one way or another to psychoanalysis. I was once a literature student and I was familiar with some of them. *The Origin of Consciousness in the Breakdown of the Bicameral Mind* by Julian Jaynes. *The Interpretation of Dreams* by Sigmund Freud. *Man and His Symbols* by Carl Gustav Jung. *The Japanese Psyche: Major Motifs in the Fairy Tales of Japan* by Hayao Kawai and Sachiko Reece. He had an eclectic taste. I liked that about him. He didn't remind me of any of my literature professors, that's another thing I liked about him.

We drove out to what the students called Mt. Adler in the range (by car five minutes away from campus). You should know Adler is one of the Santa Clarita's one hundred most famous occult sites. Adler literally meant eight peaks. Adler is the tallest standing at 2900 metres. The hills and ridges offered some extraordinary hiking, but that's not why we were there. You see, it was Jon's idea to visit all the holy mountaintop sites found in my nightmares. Why Adler? Why Marder? Why Warhola? If my memory serves me—Jon's idea was to obliterate the subconscious, nihilistic weight of these psychogeographies by confronting, cross-wiring, cross-pollinating my phantasmatic projections with the very *excesses* of the Real Adler. The Real Marder. The real Warhola. How utterly surreal, I thought. Could it work? By visiting my previously imagined psychogeographies, could I get a handle on the 'pre-logical proto-cosmic Real' thereby obliterating my bad mood, my malaise, my nightmares. I don't want to wake up in cold sweats. I was willing to try anything. I was a bit surprised that the hike was as challenging as it was. It should've taken us less than an hour from the bottom to the peak.

In my dream narrative Kathy Acker and her literary executor drag my sex-deprived corpse up the entire ascent. They covered the body in a plastic tarp. The forest floor is blanketed with a fine layer of pine needles. The mountainside is littered with tiny bits of granite. At the peak Kathy Acker chanted the Buddhist rejuvenation incantation and before their very eyes the author of *MAO PAO SAO (2009)*, and *Red Lioness, Fucking, and Post-apocalyptic, post-post modern polemics* (2007) sprang back into life. For a moment I was unable to control the movement of my flailing arms and legs. And for a second Matias Viegener thought he would have to re-kill the zombie. Kathy ordered me to lie down. I refused and Matias socked me in the face. A bummer. It left a horrible purple bruise, left eye. I eventually obliged. Matias found a rope and tied my arms and legs. Helpless, they fondled and stroked me. Kathy hyper-sensitised my nipples. Matias plunged a makeshift dildo into my bum hole. A tear ran down my cheek. As I traversed the psychic field between my superego and id, Kathy kissed me. And then slapped me across the bruised side of my face. Anxiety turned into an orgy. After an hour of this, we swapped places and Matias and I pissed all over Kathy Acker's face. Afterwards we talked about the fact that we all got off on humiliation, a sadomasochistic sensibility spurred on from our nihilistic times, the radical jouissance that gave all of our lives a sense of the 'transcendent' and phantasmatic. She asked about my childhood and I asked about hers. As we descended down the trail I could see a full moon shining above the cover of pine trees. It was late when we finally got back to the trailhead. A group of well-trained snow monkeys killed Kathy Acker. I am reminded of something Beth McNamara (the poet soccer player) told me. It was a mediated, biologically necessary but shameless response to *Pussy, King Of The Pirates* and *Blood And Guts In High School*. Matias Viegener and I said not a word to each other.

Jon Wagner complimented me on the amount of detail I'd recalled. Thank you. But I could remember dreams if the circumstances warranted it. Wagner and I paced ourselves forward, we could hear water rushing. The tall vertical ice walls were thawing. And the closer we got to the precipice, the more I began to imagine the possibilities of falling. Jon insisted that we take the south-most trail. He was told it would be an easier trail. But we soon discovered it was one of the more difficult. I could tell because it was much less crowded. He and I only passed a handful of experimental animators the entire ascent. To kill time Jon Wagner illuminated everything! He digressed — canonical nihilism and its relation to modern nihilism and its relation to high modern nihilism and its relation to the postmodern variety palimpsestised in to my dreamscape. Then he polemicised on the current state of japanese literature!

'It used to be that japanese culture was dying, if not dead. A seemingly limp corpse. You had the barbaric, dumb mastery — the kind of stubbornness in the meiji period when an aesthete would take the time to observe a japanese scroll of a seated samurai warrior in full armour and claim it as a profound form of the wild and uninhibited greek spirit of Dionysius. Blasphemous! For they misread Nietzsche but Yukio Mishima understood Nietzsche, all too well. Shame on naïve aesthetes! Today we look at that same japanese scroll and it is clear — it is undeniable that the carefully drawn sword and tanto is a manifestation of Apollonianism, order and stateliness. Absolutely nothing to do with that frenetic energy of life and the will to mastery! Arrows and banners don't impress us any longer. A set of armour with kabuto and menpo does nothing to reveal what is essential to the cultural dilemma that the japanese aesthete faces today. I say all this to highlight only this — japan will not become the next Paris or New York by constantly deferring, fondling, and sodomising the past. The past is dead because fate willed it into the grave that it resides in. Trust fate. Take it to heart. No need to conjure it back with magic haikus, dreams and memories. Sometimes art is banal.

It can be utterly mediocre. But what more can we expect? What can we possibly expect from a generation of youths that cannot appreciate the subtlety of a Yasujiro Ozu film. These new so-called artists are not artists—simply imitators, plagiarisers, simulacrum-makers unable to appreciate or contemplate the sublime. And so what? The apocalypse will come not with fire and brimstone. But with chit-chat and cherry blossoms.'

If you look at *The Physical Impossibility of Death in Someone Living* (1991) and you're not a nihilist, there's no way to see it. Forget all the hype you've been fed on the ybas: Saatchi's money, authenticity. Focus on the fourteen-foot tiger shark in formaldehyde. Is it not the perfect dovetail to death? Is it not celestial?

Consider Georges Bataille; '*Is God merely a man for whom death, or rather, thinking about death, is just one prodigious pastime?*' You still don't get it. That's okay. You're probably an unfortunate humanist. Of course not every painting or television screen or dead sheep dovetails. Is this not the point of the postmortem? '*I'm sorry, Ryu. Obviously you've worked hard on these, but in terms of innovation, major breakthroughs—I don't see it.*'

   '*—Are you going to class today?* — What for? — *Did the professor like your piece?* — No, he absolutely hated it.' Miju just lay there in her own waste; the whole world could've gone to hell and she would've asked, what for? Her perky mounds doing nothing. *The school had gotten progressively more conservative*. Her body quartered. The bed was covered. Books! Books! Everywhere! Her short black hair; her head upside down. Soft-featured, wide-eyed Miju. She eyed Ryu's books near the pool of piss—some of the covers were wet. An incomplete encyclopedia collection; *Delusion*, Frenssen and

Islam Life. A whole row as a sanctuary for good women. Sylvia Plath's *The Bell Jar*. Chris Kraus' *Video Green*. Charles Bukowski's *Women*. Charlotte Brontë's *Jane Eyre*. Jane Austen's *Emma*. Chris Kraus' *Aliens & Anorexia*. A defaced paperback copy of Emily Brontë's *Wuthering Heights*. The thought did cross her mind: *the chance of a sudden earthquake and how all the books would fall, crush her, drown her, words. What a way to go!*

'What do you think the difference is between Matias and his dalmatian?' Miju didn't have to think; she gave a typical Tokyo girl answer. *'One's happy, the other doesn't know how to be happy.'*

'The frustrating thing is—the Real. This game that the Real plays with me; of allowing me or generating in me devastating thoughts—but to then resist; for the Real to resist my Action to actualise those devastating thoughts into profound art, a good book, a sublime thing! This is maddening! The Real is crazy! It's a torture session; a cruel Master that'll give its slave a hint of pussy but only a hint.'

'But what about the MFA degree and the structures that support it? Is it not part of the Real? Isn't it the case that it is *for* thought. I am not one of those cynics that believes not in the MFA—because you know, it is exactly that void that the MFA degree castrates—if one had not produced-actualised material art or the good book. It is a consolation for not materialising those *devastating* thoughts.'

'What does this dream mean?' Jon looked at the scribblings. The red composition book. The dream was enigmatic: a man runs, the rock path made for tourists and off in the distance a vast frozen landscape filled with green, envious! His legs are like those of a well-bred racing horse; no fatigue, no ruin, no will to slowness and descent. Only the steady beautiful feeling one gets from a powerful beast. Who outruns him? A thug with a baby on his back; a tourist! But apparently he runs faster than the beast. At our destination what happens? We see those Easter Island statues, those heads, elongated heads; there must be a dozen of them! Or let's say—five dozen! Head after head as the tangerine sunset light filters through the gaps, touching the ancient hieroglyphs and totems, greek symbols, lost languages, etc, etc. None of them can I mouth. I wish I could. You'd wish too if you had the dream!

And you slip in thinking to yourself – this is amazing. A museum? Roman statuaries, giant Mayan blocks, war tools, ancient chinese rosaries, different levels of strange gold and dark pockets everywhere. On the second level you look down at a giant statue of Buddha named inappropriately Ezo and you feel the presence of the other tourist. You don't want to look the Other in the eye. You feign interest in other directions; glyphs, Ezo. And then suddenly you feel the soft skin of someone you hadn't expected. M? Yes, M.

Jon Wagner's office was just as Ryu had imagined it. To the far right corner the door and next to the red rectangle, three book shelves filled vertically with glowing corpses. You captured a glimpse of some of the titles. Freud's oeuvre in chronological order: *Die Traumdeutung, Zur Psychopathologie des Alltagslebens, Drei Abhandlungen zur Sexualtheorie, Zur Einführung des Narzißmus, Jenseits des Lustprinzips, Die Zukunft einer Illusion, Das Unbehagen in der Kultur*. Good ol' Sigmund, leather bound all for show. On the second shelf you got a better sense of Dr. Wagner's mindset. A patchwork of Lacanian and post-Lacanian thought: *The Seminar XX, Encore: On Feminine Sexuality, the Limits of Love and Knowledge,*

Subjective Experience and the Logic of the Other, The Lacanian Subject: Between Language and Jouissance, The Fragile Absolute, The Puppet and the Dwarf, Everything You Always Wanted to Know About Lacan…But Were Afraid to Ask Hitchcock. Booksbooksbooks! Jon and Ryu Asakawa, they belonged together. Two peas in a pod; one liked to preserve books, the other burned them. Both showed symptoms of the same disease: bibliomania. One secretly used the other to remedy his obsessive compulsive behaviour. The other simply feigned a remedy to disabuse himself of his tremendous guilt.

There could not have been a Christ without a St. Paul. Could the same be said for Kathy Acker? An Acker without a Matias Viegener? An Acker without a Johnny Golding? Sometimes when Johnny Free isn't talking, illuminating a stanza—one contemplates origins. Her origins. Because Johnny Free grew weary of her rut—which consisted of commuting from the crowded and foul seibu shinjuku station to a large, grey, shell-shaped, architectural abstraction (affectionately named the akagai building by her male co-workers) and then slaving feverishly in her office for the longest twelve hours any free-spirited gaijin has ever had to endure, restructuring profit guidelines and finalising licensing agreements for the morally dubious sukebe jijii corporation, after which the debased Johnny Free visits her local bar to wash down a handful of complimentary soybeans with a few flat beers, all the while knowing that she eventually has to go back to an empty home that wasn't occupied by a daughter that wouldn't talk to her, and an ex-husband that had divorced her for not working hard enough, and then of course, the proverbial sleep (where our protagonist does not dream) only to wake up the next day and repeat the process—this is the monotony, the rut, the stale drudgery she could no longer stomach—and because Johnny

*Free grew weary of it, because she was heroic enough to want
something better, to desire something real, to relish more out of
life than the strategically planned glamour of work, family, and
consumer society, because this was one human being that wasn't
going to be shat upon and end up as another victim of the
monster-monolith that was the tanshin-funin machine (like so
many of our East Asian brothers and sisters), because she could
not take the constant threat of annihilation and the utter
banality of her present circumstances—it was in that dark and
decidedly hallowed bar that she had made up her mind and
decided to write POETRY. This scenario is only one of many.
Origins. Suffice it to say this is Ryu's daydream.*

10.11am. A Thursday. An unusually cold overcast morning.
Johnny Free's poetics workshop. Butler Building 4 (in the
evening this room would be used for Thesis presentations by
Writing Program MFA candidates). I don't remember what
Johnny Free was wearing. Although, she did not resemble
them, Jen always reminded me of a cross between Malarie
Marder and Frida Kahlo. Like the Red Lioness, Johnny was
always keenly alert. Although, I had never confided in her I
always felt like I could. I never felt manipulated by her. A calm,
complex maternal presence. Ryu often wondered what she
thought of him. Perhaps nothing. Perhaps she admired his
powerful ego. Perhaps not. In my own estimation I was too
bourgeois. Always searching, desiring singularities. That one
thing. A single break, all encompassing raison d'être, a
transcendent jouissance beyond any and all experiences.
Perhaps Johnny sees this in me. From time to time I withdraw.
Ryu withdrew from the class more and more. Increasingly
separate from the group. Hopefully with a vibrant nihilism, but
all too often it was the passive kind. Ryu was sure she saw his
character flaws. His deteriorating personality. Perhaps she finds
me irritating. Boring. Perhaps in her eyes I am Sisyphus.

Endlessly reaching. Deferring. Occasionally reaching the summit. Every victory. Tainted. Pyrrhic. Lost.

I often feel like that character in *No Longer Human* by Osamu Dazai. Andrew lent me his copy. Page fifty-five haunts me. 'The masters through their subjective perceptions created beauty out of trivialities. They did not hide their interest even in things which were nauseatingly ugly, but soaked themselves in the pleasure of depicting them.'

I wonder if any of my classmates: Rene L, Joseph P, G. Canali — when they read my prose, my so-called pornography — do they get a sense of page fifty-five. Or do they see me as the consummate misogynist. I am sure Rene is staring at me. Yet I do not want to return the gaze. He is intimidating and overpowering. Where is Ryu?

Irene. Derrick. Eron. What did I have in common with these giants? This is what I wondered as they dissected, probed my carefully crafted prose. Irene. Derrick. Eron. Irene. Derrick. Eron. Irene. Derrick. Eron. Irene. Derrick. Eron. Irene sucking Derrick sucking Eron sucking Irene sucking Derrick sucking Eron fucking Irene fucking Derrick fucking Eron. Say it enough times and the names are interchangeable. Every name is the same name. Take a piece of text (Shakespeare's *Henry V*) switch the names, translate the text to your own particular socio-economic circumstances, your own interests (e.g. CalArts, East Asia). This is how you _____. Dishonor not Lynne Tillman.

As one develops a politics. As Johnny Free introduces you to more and more poetry (e.g. David Henderson, Lisa Robertson, *Occasional Work and Seven Walks from the Office for Soft Architecture*) — manufacture a politics — even if it is gestural.

Write the polemic that suits the gesture. Plagiarise. Cannibalise. Because in all likelihood you are outside of time. Tradition. History. It is a way of appropriating what is otherwise denied. As an art student you can't inherit.

Portrait of an eye

O Speaks Again

As a child my father was the consummate photographer.
Throughout my life I can distinctly remember my grey-bearded
father behind the camera lens ordering me to freeze or to sit
still. There was even a summer when my father after reading
Nihon Hyakumeizan got it into his fat head that he had to
climb Akadake and take a photo of me at its peak. His reason as
he shared it with me was that he had a dream the previous night;
a vision of me in the forefront with the mystical, snowcapped
Mt. Fuji in the distance. But I had no desire of fulfilling my
father's subconscious fantasies. At the time yes, I did have some
interest in photography. But I thought climbing a mountain
on a whim was a pointless exercise.

The night before the Akadake climb I dreamt of standing on the
edge of the summit naked, posing for the camera. I remember
that dream clearly. It felt like April and the morning was
unseasonably cold. The drive took place in the late afternoon.
Although I don't remember the entire trip I do recall seeing
flashes of familiar images as we passed them. The Tokyo towers
shimmering and cutting unmercifully into that grey, mute sky.
Fuzzy chuo sen, arrogant. Bulwarked salarymen with blank
expressions on their otherwise brilliant faces. Slippery *kogals*
with rainbow-coloured umbrellas crossing wet, depressed
intersections. Streaks of fluorescent lavender. The green
translucent millipede streaming down my passenger side
window. It's not enough to recall them. And even after I wake

up this feeling lingers, as if I left something behind by doing the unthinkable and waking up.

We trekked across Yatsugadake range. As my father simultaneously took photos of the foliage and explained to me that there were eight major peaks in the range, I secretly played with myself thinking about Hemingway. Akadake was the tallest standing a little under 3,666 metres. I didn't expect to like climbing, but in my dream narrative it all felt very familiar. Breathing in the cold mountain air. Feeling my muscles strain. I was enjoying myself. But as the day progressed I was surprised by how challenging the hike was.

To understand the significance of the above story I suggested to Dr. Asakawa that he read *The Rape of the Nation and the Hymen Fantasy: Japan's Modernity, the American South, and Faulkner* by Mizuho Terasawa and Tomoko Kuirbayashi. I had on the purple suzi watch that I wore when I was in kindergarten, strange evidence of dream logic. It took us four hours from Utsukushii no mori. As we pushed ourselves forward we could hear water rushing. The tall vertical ice walls were thawing. And the closer we got to the precipice, the more I began to imagine the possibilities of falling. It occurred to me then what it would be like to die in a dream? What would happen if I let my dream self fall off the dream rockface into the abyss? If I died here would my real self also die? Rather than finding out, my father insisted that we take the south-most trail. He was told it would be an easy trail. But we soon discovered it was one of the more difficult paths. I could tell because it was much less crowded. He and I only passed a handful of gaijin american Alpinists the entire ascent.

By late afternoon we could hear thunder in the distance. The sky darkened. Snowflakes began to fall. As the snow began to fall more heavily, it dawned on me how strange all of this was. I was in a lucid state realising that all of it: the mountain, my father, the sound of my shoes crunching into the snow, the crystallised ice on my father's beard, all of it was in fact not real. But this realisation wasn't in itself what was amazing. I had had previous dreams on countless other nights where I'd realised the obvious.

Playing numbers and meaning

The amazing thing about this particular dream was the clarity of detail I received and processed while I inhabited this dream world. Take for example my father telling me that Akadake was the tallest peak standing a little under 3,666 metres. Nevermind the fact that my dream-father got it wrong (the actual Akadake stands at 2,899 metres). But the fact that my father would give such a specific number. 3,666, this felt deliberate, as if the number was a coded message. It has meaning in it I think. Years later when I was admitted into the university, I asked Professor Asakawa (who had apparently read Freud and Jung) what he thought about it. And he told me that dreams were a result of the 'Dionysian subconscious' (a term that he had coined after reading Nietzsche and William James) and as a result much of it had to do with nymphomania or wish fulfilment. I asked him about the number 3,666. He told me he would contemplate it, but that I would figure it out soon enough.

I've known Professor Asakawa forever. A friend of the family, when my mother decided to re-marry she chose Professor Asakawa. The girls at the university didn't find him all that appealing. I on the other hand found him endlessly intriguing. I've read his biography. He is the author of *1,966 Haikus About One Thing* (1982) (a book I've read over a dozen times), published by Murakami Press; reissued in paperback with a new introduction by philosopher and cult novelist John Gill (1995). A former Yamamoto Prize Winner for his essay on the ideology of japanese landscape design, Professor Asakawa has published numerous articles on a variety of eighteenth to twentieth century topics, most recently on 'Hokusai's Nihilism' in *Cherry Blossom* (1999) and on 'Ryu Murakami and 20th-Century Gender Ideology' in *Robot Criticism* (1998). He was awarded a Guggenheim Fellowship for 1999–2000 for his book-length project, '*Problems of Oriental Representation in 20th-Century Japan and Why Shouldn't Oharu Faint?*' He offers courses in postcolonial studies, japanese literature, and twentieth-century american pornographic literature.

It was a hard climb to the base of the peak. The snow began to come down harder. The wind chilled at a rapid speed. And my ears began to ache. What made it even scarier was the nagging feeling that someone or something beyond the rocks was following us. My father told me not to worry. He assured me that it was probably a harmless snow monkey. They were apparently numerous in this part of the park.

The manifestation of O's psychosis

There were supposed to be chains and red ladders to help you at the steepest areas of the ascent, but the snow had covered the surrounding area. The hike had two false peaks and it was at the first we decided to set up camp. In the tent it dawned on me that the person I had assumed was my father all this time was actually Professor Asakawa. He was a dead ringer for the actor Ittoku Kishibe. But unlike Ittoku, Professor Asakawa had the body of a gymnast and the palest skin, almost translucent. It also dawned on me that I didn't know his first name. He told me it was Roe. Later on I found out it was Ryu. What a feeling it gave me. Wind howling outside. My stepfather and I naked, entwined, ravishing each other inside a layer of hot mass. Alone together on top of mythical Akadake. It was in this darkness with the risk of being engulfed by an avalanche that he asked me if I was a virgin. I lied. He whispered something into my ears. I asked him…

I didn't hesitate and quickly flung my legs apart. He was apparently in no hurry to plant his seeds inside me. As I tried to kiss his sex, he flinched and ordered me to lie back down on the tent floor. I obeyed. I considered kicking him off and refusing to cooperate. But I was curiously unnerved. I had never seen Professor Asakawa's dark, erotic side and I wanted to know where it would take us. Besides this was a dream. I kept reminding myself that I had nothing to lose.

That night I dreamt he ravished me. He used his belt as a blindfold and put it over my eyes and ordered me to remain still. He fingered my quim. Exposed my anus and fingered that. He poured burning lager into my dripping wet cunt and drank out of it. He spread tuna from a jewel box I was saving for later across my chest and ate off it. After awhile, our love nest began to smell foul with the intoxicating combination of alcohol, sushi, and sex. But that didn't stop the beast.

I could hear the snow storm outside worsen as he positioned me in the strangest of poses. I could feel him inside me. I was surprised by how large it was. With scientific deliberation he drew his samurai sword into my body. In and out. In and out. In and out. The whole of my body shivering, I begged him to slow down, but his deliberation only quickened. The titillation soon became unbearable as he manipulated the lager bottle along my clitoris. The blood shot into my head. I thought I would slip away from the pleasure right then and there.

He finally took off the blindfold. By this time I'd become unbearably curious about its exact length. Inside me it had to be a good seven inches. But the darkness hid his member from any scrutiny or gaze. He bent down and caressed my tuft of black hair. He kissed me on my neck and then the curve of my waist. As the storm raged all around us he asked the question. 'Would you kiss it?' I obliged.

Afterwards we settled in, unzipped the roof of the tent, and watched the clouds reveal a cheshire cat. We gazed at it. He offered me a cigarette and I took a few drags. For the first time in years I felt complete. He asked me about what I was planning to do for the summer. I told him about my father having come across *Nihon Hyakumeizan* and his obsession with taking my picture at Akadake's peak. I confided that what I really wanted to do was spend the summer at Suma Beach with Kobi and finish reading all of my Ryu Murakami novels. He was surprised that I was a Murakami fan. He probably thought I was just another city girl. He was sure that I must like Banana Yoshimoto. I did. But I made it clear to him that I was first and foremost a Murakami girl.

He asked about my aspirations and I told him that I wanted to be a writer like my mother. I also mentioned that my younger brother died at a young age. Apparently an act of suicide. I expected a reaction from the professor, but he simply nodded and listened.

I asked him about his plans and he said he was looking forward to working with my mother on an english translation of *1,966 Haikus About One Thing*. I knew that over the previous summer Professor Asakawa and my mother had worked on a translation of her first novel *14 Dead Zebras Brailled Brown*. He was also looking forward to working on a lecture series about the metaphorical significance of mountains and macaques in early twentieth century japanese literature. As he spoke I noticed how brilliant and grey his pupils were. It reminded me of two dead, science fiction moons. I could make out my reflection in them. I saw myself seeing myself. I asked Professor Asakawa about his childhood. He'd grown up in an orphanage. He told me that he and his friends shut down Tokyo university in the 1960s. May '68 was a recent event for him. I was impressed. He was part of zenkyoto, the Joint Campus Action movement. He became an only child. Every animal finds a niche or dies. His younger brother committed suicide. The college entrance exams proved too much for him.

An entry from O's secret diary

When your mother takes her own life the hardest thing to do is clean out the room she once fucked, wrote, and thought in. I suppose the fear is that you won't find any answers. And even if you do find a suicide note — will reading it make it any easier? Its been six months since her passing. And I have yet to clean out her desk. My stepfather volunteered to do it, but I felt that my mother would've wanted me to. I'm not sure why I've been putting it off.

O's return to the fantasy narrative

As we got better acquainted I felt less guilty about the whole affair. The remainder of our time in the tent was not wasted. We spent hours attempting to fuse our fleshy mouths together into one writhing, ecstatic chunk of organica. Exchanging our saliva. Him tasting me. Me tasting him. As the moonlight glistened off my chest and legs he began to kiss my thighs knowingly, inevitably leading to my sex. But before he could go at it, we were interrupted by a series of awkward steps crunching on the snow outside.

From a distance it looked like the silhouette of a small boy and for a moment I thought it was my brother returned from the grave. But this wasn't the case. As the silhouette drew closer, we saw that it wasn't a boy. It wasn't my dead brother. It was the anti-metaphor. A red-faced, red-bottomed japanese macaque with unusually large pink genitals. My first instinct was to run away but I hesitated fearing I would freeze to death. I ran. My irrational fear was that the animal would rape me. It was unmercifully cold, but all I wanted to do was abandon Professor Asakawa and run. I ran up the precipice and to my surprise I saw in the vast distance a billowing Mt. Fuji ready to erupt. Behind me I heard Professor Asakawa scream in horror. I could only assume that the monkey had bitten off his member.

In the light of the morning of the world

In the morning I half expected to see Professor Asakawa castrated and writhing in pain. But he was outside unburdening himself. I don't know how I got back to the tent. It all looked so unfamiliar. The storm had stopped and I saw the most beautiful view of the southern alps and Fuji-san. The far-off summit was topped with a brilliant ivory. How different the view looked from the previous night! Mt. Fuji did appear as a familiar metaphor. If I close my eyes now I can still see the pink morning clouds casting large blue shadows on the mountain's symmetrical, snowcapped cone. It was unnerving. But also inexhaustibly beautiful in its grandeur. The summit made completely invisible by the crust of the pale pink shroud. And as I breathed out, I thought I saw it billowing again. For a moment that felt like an infinity, I didn't understand my place in such a chaotic landscape.

Professor Asakawa had relieved his first name in the snow. He looked out at the view. Took a moment to take in the sun and warned me that the metaphor would erupt one day. After its long period of dormancy it couldn't help but ejaculate. He warned me that it would happen soon and that I wouldn't be safe. Not even in Tokyo.

Giving up the postmodern ghost

To end with transformations. Karen Eliot decided to
appropriate that which was otherwise denied. Adorno and
Heidegger. Their appetites had contaminated my previously
stable worldview. Her idea: perhaps they had the answers to
snap me out of this zombie state, this undead state. To unveil
the utopia that was ready to explode at any moment.
Everywhere Karen Eliot looks there are orange peels, condoms,
rubble sidewalks, steel cranes and exposed wires threatening
to evaporate my tourist-gaze. Karen Eliot's advice to me was
simple: you have to work with trash, pit it against itself. My
reply: if you say so.

I met Karen Eliot at a last-minute Neoist Apartment Festival.
19 February 2008. 11.15pm. Nearly a full moon. She was out
on the balcony, smoking, gazing at the sparkling sky line. It
was nothing compared to the view of Los Angeles from Matias'
bachelor pad. From behind she looked like Sylvia Beach
wearing a leather jacket. Awkward pretty legs. The nervous
energy was palpable. You have a light? Her lively, sharply
sculptured face reminded me of Adelle Stripe's. We talked.
Exchanged emails. She was apparently from North Yorkshire
from a poor working class background. She told me about the
bands she was into as an angst-ridden teenager: *The Slits, The
Cramps, The Normal, King Tubby, The Gun Club…* I hadn't
a clue about any of them. I told her about the bands I was into
in the mid nineties: *Bratmobile, Bikini Kill, Thee Headcoatees,
Black Flag, The Descendents…* She hadn't a clue. We decided
to play it safe and we agreed only to talk about *The Smiths*. I

admitted I was never a big fan of Morrissey. I found his songs sappy and disengenuous. She exploded. She half-heartedly conceeded to the second point, but she defended his lyrics. *Jeane / The low-life has lost its appeal / And I'm tired of walking these streets / To a room with a cupboard bare / Jeane / I'm not sure what happiness means / But I look in your eyes / And I know / That it isn't there / Punctured bicycle / On a hillside desolate / Will nature make a man of me yet? / When in this charming car / This charming man / Why pamper life's complexities / When the leather runs smooth / On the passenger seat?* Alienated. Disenchanted. How many other Karen Eliots had I met in the past?

Of course Karen Eliot isn't the name on her NHS donor card. Karen Eliot is a multiple-use name that anyone is welcome to use for activist and artistic endeavour. It was developed in order to counter the male domination of the Neoist movement, the most predominant multiple use-names being Monty Cantsin, Luther Blissett and Mister Trippy. The CalArts equivalent became Bridghe Mullins, Reena Spauling, Kathy Acker, Michelle Lee, Janice Lee, Christine Wertheim, etc. Maxi Kim is a multiple-use name that anyone is welcome to use for otaku activist and otaku artistic endeavour. It was developed in order to counter the predominant literary attitudes within the University of California. Gina Clark is a multiple-use name developed in order to counter aesthetic attitudes generated in 2007 — what later became known as the year of alienation. Two hundred and eighty seven days have passed since Gina Clark's *Flicking the Tit of the Weeping Lemur,* and still these Goldsmiths kids ask me to give my detailed account of the experience which has been considered a utopia, an act of utopic performativity. The alienation is quite palpable here in London; this is how I account for all of the interest in *Flicking the Tit.* Of course the problem wasn't an ism (as it was in the states);

it had to do with what my dear *other mother*, Chris Kraus calls *the neocorporate neoconceptual*. Enter Damien Hirst's shiny diamond-encrusted skull.

What does London want? What is it that Londoners want? Meanwhile: What does Tokyo want? What does Los Angeles want? What does any blossoming victim of some externally imposed 'situation' want? Karen asked the questions I could not answer. I couldn't understand the question. And I was freezing. It was nearly two months and I still hadn't gotten used to the Jack-the-Ripper weather. Inside young artists from Goldsmiths and the Old Royal Naval College were shaving their legs, recreating Clark's April 2007 performance-installation. It was quite a party. I was immediately taken back to the CalArts days. At the centre of the performance artist's site of ritual and renewal we find a large occult-like circle drawn out with toothpaste. At the entrance toothbrushes and toothpaste are provided. At the northwest stand razors are provided. Here spectators are invited to become participants. Here one is even tempted to say—*ah, a micro-permanent autonomous zone where our daily routines, body works and the everyday are revalued*. But of course aspects of such a space are much more refined, complicated. Consider the layered soundscape: in the northeast corner the atmospheric pounding of nails, possible evidence of a torture session. To the northwest: near-ambient winds, haunted unintelligible talk. And in the southwest corner: a myriad of phantasmagoric german aphorisms, sparse nostalgic piano playing and echos.

Was she thirsty? Beck's or cheap red wine? I suggested we go downstairs to my room. She liked that the narrow window and door frames were painted Clementine-orange. She was surprised by the few books and albums. I reminded her I'd only been in the uk since New Year's Day. My table: a tangle of rubber bands, ten pences, stacks of magazines and papers on stacks of takeaway boxes. She picked up a marked copy of the book you are currently holding in your hand. Mister Trippy had gone over it with a fine-tooth comb. Have you ever met Mister Trippy? I was surprised by the question. Given her interest in Neoism, I had assumed she'd known the author of *Down & Out in Shoreditch and Hoxton*. That's one of my favourites! He had signed my copy: *For Maxi on our first edit meeting, One Break is a fabulous book. Keep on bumpin'! Mister Trippy 17/01/08.*

What's he like? Quite the opposite of what I expected. I had been told by the writer Amy Prior that he was an intimidating, no-nonsense skinhead. He was a teddy bear. Apparently it was all just a stage persona. It was the same with Sylvère Lotringer. I was expecting an emotionally exhausted nihilist. This was the impression I got from Chris Kraus' books. He was the very opposite. How did you meet him? I was Chris' assistant for a time; this was in the beginning of the year of alienation. Sylvère was in Baja and Chris was very generous, she urged me to go down. For three days I had the privilege of watching Mister Black pry open the clams he'd caught the twilight before last. He was sun and sea-burned, happy. As the french philosopher attempted to insert a knife into a particularly difficult gap, he explained to me the central problem with my favorite Lacanian-Marxist. — *Yes, he's entertaining—I've seen his lecture. He's even insightful, but he's not very difficult. Deleuze and Guattari: they're real thinkers. After you read their books, you're not quite sure where you are. But with Žižek—there's no difficulty, no challenge. Ah, this clam just doesn't want to open.*

It didn't take Karen long to skim through the book you are currently holding in your hand. You're not expecting a shag. Are you? I convinced her that the book was just a book. I was neither Ryu nor Kato nor Miju nor Janine… I wasn't expecting oral stimulation. What was the fascination with pornography? Masturbation? I threw the question back at her. I recall having a similar conversation with the working philosopher Gauti Sigthorsson. From the perspective of the student, what is it about professors and intellectuals in general that jumpstarts the libido? It was all a matter of knowledge; not simply a matter of obtaining it or gaining mastery over it, but to be seduced by it, to be enmeshed, entangled, made interchangeable by the unattainable. And it is important that it remains unattainable. As soon as one actualises the fantasy, all is lost. Thoreau ultimately understood that eating wild animals did not in fact result in his own transcendent transformation. And the same goes with Miju and Ryu. Eating each other out will not result in the merging of two knowledge sets.

Karen came across some of my MA—phD course notes concerning Adorno and Heidegger. They were scattered and embarassing. Picture badly drawn cones, cubes, three dimensional puzzle pieces with arrows zig zagging this way and that. Hastily written phrases such as: *REINSCRIPTION OF BEING = PHILOSOPHER'S GOD, FULLY UNIFIED SUBJECT = DESCARTES' PHILOSOPHY, WHAT DOES IT MEAN NOT TO BELONG? A = A = A TECHNOLOGY IS CATEGORISATION—OBLIVION NEEDS FORGETTING—REVELLING NEEDS FORGETTING—FOUCAULT + DELEUZE + NIETZSCHE = EASILY EXPLOITABLE MIXTURE, TRUE AESTHETIC CONSEQUENCES VS. AESTHETIC ATTITUDES, THEORY + CURRICULUM + GRADES = TECHNOCRATIC ADMINISTRATION OF ART / JOHNNY: YOU CAN'T HAVE ONE LONG ORGASM / HOW DOES MOURNING END? THE BREAK HAS TO BE*

CATASTROPHIC / THE ARRIVAL VS. THE STEPBACK / FOUND TIME = IDENTITY/HOW DO YOU ARRIVE? HOW DO YOU KNOW YOU'VE ARRIVED? STUDY THE LAW = GO THROUGH THE PROCESS / REARRANGING THE CHAIRS ON THE TITANIC/b = B/WHEN DOES THE ARTWORK WORK? / WHEN IS SOMETHING FINISHED?

We're still in my flat. I'm sitting at my desk. Karen has the nervous habit of crossing and uncrossing her leg as she eats. She is sitting on the bed. We've ordered some Indian takeout. We're sharing a set meal with chicken tikka and bhuna with mushroom rice and potatoes on the side. Finding Heidegger senseless and unresisting, Adorno tore down his pants, thus laying Heidegger's secret places open to his hands and eyes. Heidegger endured this without flinching, till emboldened by his sufferance and silence, Adorno attempted to lay him down on the settee, and Heidegger felt Adorno's hand on the lower part of his naked thighs. Heidegger hurriedly crossed his legs. While unbuttoning his filthy tweed breeks, Adorno attempted to force Heidegger's legs apart with his knee. Heidegger struggled and was losing ground when the brute gave up the fight, cursing the fact that he suffered from premature ejaculations. A month of mulling over *Negative Dialectics* and this shabby rendition was the anti-intellectual end point.

Only a Karen Eliot could console me at a time like this. She suggested that I was on the right path; however, rather than attempting to take a side on the whole object-subject debate, she advised me to simply take stock of those attitudes and movements that would help the practice of emerging artists. So rather than trying to figure out whether or not Heidegger's ontology relapsed into a stubborn idealism, simply internalise Adorno's criticism of the ideology of 'authenticity'

95

(*Eigentlichkeit*). Rather than trying to figure out if it is even possible to develop a philosophy beyond subject and object, simply internalise Adorno's weariness of absolute principles and notions which privilege subjectivity. Rather than taking a side on the neo-Kantian revival debate, simply internalise the fact that the 'ontological need' is the desire to break out of traditional philosophy. Rather than attempting to read Adorno as a student of Nietzsche, simply internalise the fact that the totality of this world is not and never will be appropriate. So rather than introducing the theory of value or commodity fetishism, simply internalise Adorno's criticism of identity thinking, or reification. Bollocks to dogmatism! Bollocks to pure epistemology!! Bollocks to philosophy itself!!!

2.15am. Karen Eliot is on her back. I'm on my back as well. We're almost through with the green bottles of Beck's. She's hogging all the pillow. She's reading the cover story of the most recent *Metro: Town's toll of suicide hits 17 / A TEENAGE girl yesterday became the 17th young person to be found dead in Wales' Bridgend area, which has been blighted by suicides.* Was there any hope of utopia in the short twenty-first century? I invited Karen to a one-day University of Greenwich conference on the topic of trouble-making in the academy. I loved the title of the conference: *Trouble Makers / Making Trouble.* Speakers included Gary Hall, John Hutnyk and James Swinson. I was to give a very short talk entitled *Giving up the Postmodern Ghost.* Where will it be held? The Old Royal Naval College. I described the new utopia as the philosopher artist Johnny Golding described it to me: it was a magic garden, an instance where the forgotten had inherited the palace. And walking around the village it was quite obvious that the school was the place to be. Rumours abounded that the school was built by Christopher Wren as a hospital for lunatic mariners. I could not help but think of CalArts; many had circulated the myth that the Disney experiment was previously an asylum for the criminally insane.

What would be the topic of my talk? I got off the bed and went through the book you are currently holding in your hand. 'I'm not sure. I'll probably begin by reading excerpts from *One Break*. Any suggestions?' 'Start with an incantation!' 'An incantation?' Begin the process that I had started in the states. And so it began: the slow and challenging process of redefining the future, reimagining utopia itself. The new multiple use-names, so far: Alev Adil, Nathalie Bikoro, Amy Prior, Shigeko Sky, Hannah Lammin, Susana Medina, Steve Peacock, Stuart Inman, Ben Myers, Bex Muirhead, Noel Campbell, Jacob Wren, John Hutnyk, Adrian Shaw, Daniel Furlani, Doug Stuart, Stamatia Portanova, Tessie Home, Paul Filmer, D.J. Tomoki, Gary Hall, Chickedy & McGuffin, Le Tetsuo, David Choe, Dave Miller, Steve Sutton, James Swinson, Adrian Tomine, Steve Beard, S. Kon, Y. Nara, A. Weerashethakul, D. Shrigley, Joseph Ushigale, Gauti Sigthorsson, Ezekial Alexander, Eishi Takaoka, Miss Sills, John & Jehn, Christine & Sammy, Big M, G & S, Steve Kennedy, Johnny Golding…

Before the days of revelation

Because I wished to alleviate myself of a childhood prejudice,
I became an english major. Like my mother I loathed european
and american literature. I explained this to Yoshi as we stewed
in one of the natural hot springs nestled between the ice-
covered mountains in Nagano prefecture. The snow monkey
didn't seem to care all that much about what I had to say. He
was more focused on the task of grooming my long black hair.
It occurred to me that I didn't know all that much about him so
I asked about his childhood and he danced around the subject
as if he'd been abused. I was more than happy to soak in the
one hundred degrees fahrenheit monkey-poop infested soup
all day, but he brought me here for a reason and I was beginning
to lose my patience.

I was lulled into a deep sleep as Yoshi caressed my hair. That
afternoon I dreamt of climbing Rateyama with my stepfather
and Professor Asakawa. I'd known in advance that one could
take a train then a cable car to Bijodaira. I took great care to
write down all the information. From Bijodaira you could take
a highland bus from the half-way point and get nearly to the
top of Mt. Tateyama. From Murodo one could take a ride in
the tunnel trolley bus and end up on the other side of Tateyama.
From Daikanbo you used a ropeway to descend down to
Kurobedaira. And from there a ride inside a cable car and a
short walk leads you to Kurobedam. From there a trolley bus
ride and with any luck you would be on the shadow side of
Mt. Akazawadake. You're now inside of Nagano prefecture
territory.

But we didn't take the multi-transportation route. No, that would've been too easy. Instead Professor Asakawa and Professor Nakamura were adamant that we maintain a level of authenticity, so we opted to do it the old-fashioned way. Step by agonising step I increasingly came to resent them. As Professor Asakawa explained it—Tateyama was one of the three most sacred mountains in japan. And I was supposed to be grateful for having the honour of climbing it as nineteenth-century patrons did. The temperature was below twelve degrees centigrade and of all the emotions I was feeling the least of them was gratitude. Rather than passing the tourist-crowded Murodo station we took a laborious secret passage that was according to Professor Asakawa developed by a high-ranking gaijin freemason in the late nineteenth century.

As we got to the steepest portions of the route I noticed a series of sacred makeshift huts. Apparently passers-by were supposed to rest a rock on top of each roof to appease the mountain gods. Normally, I wasn't very superstitious but the huts were shrouded with white mist which gave it all a supernatural quality. Also, what Professor Asakawa had said before that this mountain was one of the three most sacred, had gotten to me. As we got closer to the top we arrived at a Shinto shrine. Professor Nakamura paid 1500 yen for the three of us to enter (500 yen each). Although we paid a fee to enter the holy place, this didn't affect my predisposition to experiencing a spiritual awakening. Perhaps it was the sip of Omiki, blessed sake. Or maybe it was the sight of holy men in their brilliant orange garb. Whatever it was I felt myself lifted by that shrine. As I walked out to take the main trail to the highest point of Tateyama I was a new wo/man. It was a subtle difference, but a definite change. Everything took on a visual halo and I wasn't the only one experiencing it. Had the Buddhists spiked the sake? Professor Nakamura noted how holy the thick fog looked against the shadow side of Tateyama. Professor Asakawa was fixated by the giant rocks on the green and white patches of the summit. He kept asking my stepfather and me whether we too saw the holiness in those glowing hunks of earth, to which we nodded yes. Everything was holy that afternoon. But the magic did not last long, so we decided to descend the other side of Tateyama and call it a day.

We found ourselves in a small, seemingly traditional ryokan where all the maids had white-face and wore modern black kimonos. The sight was quite jarring. When I was eight I remember spending time at a similar ryokan in the Hokuriku area of the Ishikawa prefecture. No one there had illusions of being geisha. This was the location for Yamashiro hot spring, a relatively well-known vacation destination with a 1200-year-old history. Staying there I had the illusion of being transported to the times of antiquity. I recall a seated japanese macaque dressed as a samurai warrior in full armour. But to this day no one who was with me remembers it. At the time my brother thought it was a ghost or a demon. But even with these occasional hauntings I had enjoyed myself at Hokuriku. The ryokan meals were excellent local kaga dishes. And miso soup. They were served on wajima lacquer ware and cute kutani-yaki earthware. The Hotel Hirayukan is another special ryokan I have vivid memories of staying in. It was located somewhere in the japan alps region of northern Gifu. The rotemburo was even more memorable. Constructed from stone, the outdoor landscape made it absolutely perfect. And the bath was amazing, it was constructed from cypress trees. I remember soaking in the water and drinking in the gorgeous arched roof, while my little brother tickled my feet and grinned with glee.

Before we ate dinner, Professor Asakawa suggested that we take a communal dip in the rotemburo. I wasn't expecting much but the outdoor bath was a trip. The peaceful natural setting of the countryside adding greatly to the experience. As I stewed in the hot water Professor Asakawa talked about James Joyce's *Ulysses*. I think he knew I had skipped class. I suppose he wanted to make me feel guilty.

I couldn't follow the thread of Professor Nakamura's argument so I didn't try. I just soaked in that hot bubbling water. Then Professor Asakawa asked if I felt like fucking and I said yes. I didn't know the other middle-aged men in the outdoor bath so I took Professor Asakawa and Professor Nakamura into the sauna for a bit of privacy. Once inside I knelt and invitingly opened my mouth. I suppose I was their jissom depository. And they furiously punished their meat-sticks as if they were angry with them. My tongue undulating, Professor Asakawa came all over my face. He had no aim. His white ropes intertwined in my hair. And then my stepfather as if aroused by Professor Asakawa's initiative, shot his load all over my visage too. I got off on the fact that my face alone could arouse such uninhibited passion in these middle-aged academics. They loved the kogal look. I can't forget the fantastic expression on Professor Asakawa's face as the blood shot into his cock. It was a look of pure, unadulterated ecstasy. As the millipede trickled down my neck, I ordered both men to lick my secret abyss and both gaily obliged. At first my stepfather felt some trepidation, but he was quickly won around. Both men went to town. The pleasure was intoxicating. After the session my stepfather and I smoked cigarettes outside.

After the days of revelation

If it were any other night I would've felt myself ecstatically and steadily possessed by the Kyoto landscape — the whole blossom saturated geography, I know it to have been culled from a *classic*, some magical, inexplicable tome that shouldn't have been written (because the assumption is that only properly sacred gods have access to the disposition and seashore confidence to imagine such things). This is what Miju tells me, this is her belief not mine. She's obviously a romantic. I gave up the disease when she gave up on me. Humans and humans alone are capable of accomplishing, building all kinds of minor miracles. The Imperial Palace. Nijo castle. Sanjusangendo, the ancient temple in eastern Kyoto which is famous for its one thousand and one statues of Kannon, the goddess of mercy. The Golden Pavilion. Himeji castle. And inside these castles, palaces and even inside the smaller temples and hot springs and hidden places — we have authors (the true gods and goddesses, I think) and their brilliance. *The Tale of Genji. The Pillow Book of Sei Shonagon. Yoshida Kenko's Essays in Idleness. The Love Suicide at Amijima by Chikamatsu Monzaemon.* I'll stand before these monuments and time itself will awaken, evaporate, and vanish. They intoxicate me. Like Miju's mere presence, these books have a hold on me. If only I could write like Murasaki Shikibu. If only I had Ryu Murakami's genius. If only I had Mishima's passion. Endo's stamina. Basho's giant phallus.

'Where are your _____?' I asked.
'It doesn't work like that.'
'Why not?'

Miju looked at me. 'You're too impatient. You have to let them find you.'

'I know. I thought japan would help me. But nothing happens.'

'Don't worry. It'll come. Be patient. Look around you. Chance. Indeterminacy. Your art is what finds you.'

April in Kyoto is a good substitute for time in Tokyo, the explosion of Hiragana graphics, moving colours, and neon signifiers traded in for the pink cherry-tree blossoms along river banks and clean mountainsides draped with ancient weeping trees. Right before my eyes, the transformation of the city into countryside. Profound, yes? But I found it odd that the geographical transformation had not reflected, oscillated, permeated, hurried past into the psychogeographies of the japanese that came here to Maruyama park to enjoy the sake and the blossoms and the geishas. All had an intoxicating scent and flowed at the patrons' whim. But somehow the spectators who filled the Pontocho theater to gaze at the geisha performance at the Kamo river dance—lacked the scent. Essence. A full, substantial uncanniness. Tokyo crowds. Salarymen. College students. They all seemed out of place. It wasn't so much that they acted like tourists or even that they, for me, symbolised the literary notion of 'the collective' but the fact that they disrupted my daydream, my idleness, my fantasy of Kyoto with their loudness and dull faces and concreteness. It irritated me. They resembled spies, they knew all too well about their debilitating affects on my happy intoxication.

Enough of this. Meanderings. Why had I come to japan? What was I _____? Why? It's been so long since I've thought about these questions. They're almost meaningless now. All I had to show for my enthusiasm was grief. So I thought going away, on Miju's suggestion, would be my ticket. How naïve I was. I am still. Even as I walk behind Miju, following her steps, admiring her naked ankles, the valleys of her feet, the contours of her legs following the Kamo river I still believe in all earnestness that I can capture the sense of mystery of the sublime and the beautiful with _____. Mere _____. I've been in japan for a year and I still cannot capture it. Every day I sit down at my _____ and I spend the whole day _____. On good days I can finish _____. Of course, most of it had to be thrown away. Today was a bad day. How downtrodden am I? I look in the mirror and I see a nippon version of Sisyphus. Even in college Miju told me your art is what finds you. In retrospect I should've listened to her. I believed with a passion that I could find it. But here I am now at the precipice of my birth. Kyoto. With nothing to show for my passion, but _____. All of it is inspired. All of it deserves notice. But none of it does a _____ make. None of it did I originally intend. I showed Miju the skimpy _____ I had churned out in the morning and I could tell she was disappointed.

'What happened to you?' Miju asked. 'You were once a _____. You knew how to _____.'
'Why do you say that?' I asked. I was devastated.

'The theme of the present being swallowed up by an imaginary, never-arriving future. Mock _____. The rubric of imminent catastrophe. The _____ as the necessary mode of transcendence.'
'What?'
'It is all so plagiarised.'
'But it's all true.'
'Is it?'
'Where are your _____?' I asked again, 'you promised them.'

'You know it doesn't work like that.'
'And why not?'

Couldn't she have feigned interest? Feigned pleasure in the face of mediocrity? Spared my fragile ego? No. After all, isn't that what you do with a friend (even your mediocre _____ that have delusions of grandeur)? No. She was either too honest or too cruel. And at that moment I began to realise the answer to my question. Why did I _____? It was for her. Every thing. Every word. Every pause. Every _____. Every paragraph. Every chapter. Every thing was for her, and she understood this too well. Nihilism was always just a cover.

Miju _____. I met her in grad school. We were both getting our _____. In college no one took me seriously. I made the most audacious of literary arguments. Miju was the only person who found me amusing. My professors were never amused. Once, I was asked by a Professor Head—if I knew as he knew—the secret literary link that united Gogol, Hegel, Nietzsche, Hume, Kant, Celine and Dostoevsky. Quite unexpectedly, I took him by surprise and said yes. I said, 'My father.' He didn't understand so I explained. You see like Gogol my father pissed. Like Hegel my father enjoyed eating three meals a day. Like Nietzsche my father slept at night. Like Hume my father was witness to many sublime things. Like Kant my father bathed. Like Celine my father bled. Like Dostoevsky my father fucked on occasion. And like Marx my father read. Like a machine, the bibliomaniac read all through the night. The professor was not amused.

I wanted to _____ for all the wrong reasons. I wanted to prove to the Professor Katos of the world that I was to be taken seriously. I wanted so much for Miju to see me as more than just an amusing fool. A genius. Money. A quiet loft in matsuyama. _____ fame. I had betrayed myself. And I was only _____, about to turn _____ in five hours. It was my fourth attempt at finishing my _____. I was terrified and lonely and desperate. Miju I think sensed this, which is why she insisted that we get out of the city. Relax in the teahouses. Enjoy the cherry blossoms. The geishas. Hopefully seeing young couples walking alongside the river that mirrored the restaurants and geisha quarters, all of this was to inspire me. To deliver me from the brothel of despair I'd grown so fond of over the last few days.

There's something about the Kamo river. It had a brilliance about it. The white sand. Clear waters. The fragrant air. We came here to escape Tokyo's bad air and madness. Nestled inside a sleepy fishing village at the very tip of the peninsula, Kamo's water led us away from the tourists and salarymen. As Miju and I walked and talked on the sand barefoot admiring each other's footprints—following, criss-crossing each other's paths we could hear two loud boys splashing and jumping off a bridge. In the distance there they were. We made out youthful figures in the emerald green water with heaving masses of thunderclouds as a backdrop. The sun had gone down, but there was still some residual sashimi, pink light that gave everything a magical quality. That abundance of shimmering light. The quiet roar of endless waves. To this day I can't think of anything as beautiful or as right. Of course, this is a hyperbole. I can think of one thing.

The _____. Why am I so enamoured by it? Why do I constantly and so pathetically return to it? On second thought, it wasn't just for Miju. That's absurd. I've asked myself this often and every time I think I have a definite solution to the puzzle, the solution along with any conceivable mastery evaporates. I ask myself this now as I'm writing this sentence and sitting next to Miju on her tatami mat as the world's about to come _____. A better question—why *was* I so enamoured by it? What was the initial reason, the initial vision for my first attempt at the _____? It wasn't money. In college the idea of the starving artist appealed to me. I can't help but feel that my interest in writing is in some preternatural way linked, connected with japanese literature and has very much to do with my fascination with art. The Imperial Palace. Nijo castle. Sanjusangendo. The Golden Pavilion. Himeji castle. As a gaijin I can't help but point to the fact that these things should not _____. I initially felt it in my bones. But in point of fact they do.

I first saw her sitting cross-legged on the floor in Rivera Library in the japanese lit section. Noticed her mohawk—like Brody Armstrong's. Books around her. Shinzaburo Iketani. Nobuko Yoshiya. Chiyo Uno. Kokuseki Oizumi. Kansuke Naka. Kiku Amino. Ken (Takeru) Inukai. Kosaku Takii. Yuriko Chujo. Shiro Ozaki. Chiaki Shimomura. Jiro Sekiguchi. Shinichi Makino. Banka Fukunaga. Jitsuzo Shiraishi. Genkichi Hosoda. Tamiki Hosoda. Saburo Okada. Murao Nakamura. Kamenosuke Mizumori. Takeo Kato. Sakujiro Kano. Taizo Soma. Jun Tanaka. Zenzo Kasai. Koji Uno. Seiji Tanizaki. Kazuo Hirotsu. Yuzo Yamamoto. Musoan Takebayashi. Saisei Muro. Seikichi Fujimori. Kiyoshi Eguchi. Hyakken Uchida. Kichiji Nakatogawa. Mosaku Sasaki. Masajiro Kojima. Kyota Mizuki. Haruo Sato. Yuzuru Matsuoka. Masao Kume. Yoshio Toyoshima. Kan Kikuchi. Ryunosuke Akutagawa. Kojin Karatani's *Origins of Modern Japanese Literature.* Kathy Acker's *Pussy, King of the Pirates* (turned to page 112–113). *The Anthology of Ten Thousand Leaves.* Aren't you the girl in Professor Kato's class? Aren't you the boy with the father?

Miju was the one that recommended Barthes' *Empire of Signs*. It was a translated copy by Richard Howard and even though I had a japanese last name I had never thought about my japanese past. I found myself trapped initially by Barthes' texts, but after the second read it was as if the gordian knot in my head had loosened. Of course, it was not fully untangled (evidenced by my eventual presence in japan) but it was enough for me to believe that it could be _____. The mystery that was my past could be understood, spotlighted without shadow. Without omission. Without the help of a cheating blade.

In retrospect I was better back then. Not so much in my _____ prowess or in actual ability, but my enthusiasm, my sense of _____ could not be matched. Of course, as a freshman the university served the conventions of social realism and high modernism. Theodore Dreiser's *Sister Carrie*. James Joyce's *Ulysses*. Books I couldn't relate to. Books I didn't want to relate to. But Miju's book. Barthes' *Empires Of Signs* afforded me the kind of hope that promised not only the possibility of certain truths, but the possibility of transcending those truths. Perhaps even transcending transcendence itself. Here is where the seed, the thought that I could and ought to _____ was nurtured. Perhaps here is where the artistic act became a necessity.

    'Do you remember the first time we _____?'
    'No.' I lied.
    'You should know I liked you better back then. Not so much because you could write, but there was a naïveté about you. You weren't so preoccupied with _____ back then. The preoccupation was with life. You were interested in not failing to _____. You ask me—where are the _____? You had them back then.'

Two more hours and I would turn _____. Yukio Mishima had two successful novels published and was a celebrity at the age of twenty-four. The two boys had left and the unusually large, full moon pulsated close to the horizon. A million stars shimmered.

'My dreams,' I said to Miju, 'I don't know them any more.'
'I know,' she said. 'It doesn't matter.'
'They're your dreams too,' I said.

Later on we went down to the beach. We could see the himeji castle at the end of it. We sat down and watched the waves rolling in as the sun set. We had the beach all to ourselves and although it was warm, I pressed myself against Miju. Soon we were in each other's arms, rolling around on the pebbles. It wasn't long before her jeans were around her ankles. I was determined to get her pregnant. It was incredible, the sound of the ocean pounding in my ears and a vast expanse of thin cloud undulating in a darkened sky.

After that we just lay together on the beach for a very long time. We didn't think of putting on our clothes. We let the ocean take them.

The daughter of Miju & Ryu Asakawa

It was a lovely night, so warm that she threw her coat over her arm, and did not even put her silk scarf round her throat. As she strolled home, smoking her cigarette, two young men in evening dress passed her. She heard one of them whisper to the other, 'That is Tomi Asakawa.' She remembered how pleased she used to be when she was pointed out, or stared at, or talked about. She was tired of hearing her own name. She didn't want to be known as the love child of the late chief curators of Zerbrochen in Tokyo. There was nothing charming about murder suicide. She had often told the girl whom she had lured to love her that she was cursed, and the girl had believed her. What a laugh she had! Just like a thrush singing. The 'what if?' had bothered her for as long as she could remember. Perhaps there was no curse. Perhaps out of some deep recognition one could find happiness. And unconditional love. She was 19. Still a naïf. A bibliomaniac. Heavily invested in bibliomancy (like her mother), the occult use of books for divination. As her life slipped through her fingers, she was attempting to write something. The exegesis of her father's life. Or the exegesis of her mother's. It was Tomi's claim that all books were essentially of the same strange narrative. The rape-revenge narrative. She desired to cannibalise every book she could touch. The process was an exhausting one.

Lying on her couch she could hear the rain and the LA traffic below. She began to think over some of the things that Uncle

Kato had said to her. Was it really true that you could never escape your fate? She felt a wild longing for the unstained purity of the void. She knew even at her young age that she had tarnished herself, filled her mind with corruption and given horror to her fancy; that she'd had an evil influence on others (like her father), and experienced terrible joy as a result; and that of the countless lives that had crossed her own it had been the fairest and the most full of promise that she had brought to ruin. But was it all irretrievable? Was there no hope for her? She had read somewhere that Sylvia Plath had ended it by sticking her head in a gas oven. She thought the method was suitable, but her tiny loft apartment in Little Tokyo didn't have a gas oven. She looked around her apartment. On the book shelf a copy of *Japanese Death Poems: Written by Zen Monks and Haiku Poets on the Verge of Death*. Henry Scott Stokes' *The Life and Death of Yukio Mishima*. Of course! Ritualised suicide by seppuku. Romantic. Heroic. Why hadn't she thought of it before? It was fitting. She was born in japan, after all. Having recited one of Sant ka's haikus, she knelt and took a deep breath. *Going Deeper*. Concentrated. *And Still Deeper*. Breathed out. *The green mountains*. And plunged the paring knife into her mid-section.

Her efforts betrayed her. The dull blade pathetically ricocheted off her stomach leaving a puny scratch. She had underestimated the upperbody strength necessary to perform ritual seppuku. She looked at the cover of the book. She envied Mishima. He had chiselled biceps. Ah! in what a monstrous moment of pride and passion she had prayed that the portrait of Tomi Sasahara should bear the burden of her days, and she keep the unsullied splendour of eternal doubt! All her failure had been due to that. Better for her that the sins of her parents had brought a sure, swift penalty. There was a purification in punishment. Not 'Forgive us our sins' but 'Smite us for our iniquities' should be the prayer of artists to a most just God. Demoralised, she drove to Vroman's on Colorado Blvd, famed as Southern California's largest and oldest independent book store.

Across the street from Vroman's is a decent sushi place. There's not a lot about Los Angeles that one can love. The dull weather. The duller residents. The traffic. Hyper-gentrification. Commodities. Merchants. It was all a nightmare. But if there is one thing it is the sushi. Good sushi at the place across from Vroman's. It was the same 'sushi bar in Pasadena' where the initial *I Love Dick* 'situation' occurred between Dick _____, Sylvère Lotringer and Chris Kraus. She had a bottle of Ginjo-shu, a premium sake brewed using highly polished rice, and fermented at colder than usual temperatures. Light, aromatic, and fruity. If she'd known she was ever going to write about that night, she'd have noted what she had with the sake. Probably some kind of suzuki (sea bass) along with temaki sushi, hand-rolled cones of fish, rice, and vegetables. Whatever she had that night, she knew she didn't have wasabi or soy sauce on the side. She always made it a point to eat it naked. Better for her palate. After the meal, she ordered some California rolls and spicy tuna rolls to take away, left them in her car and walked into Vroman's.

It's a big book store. It's as large as the famous City Lights Books in San Francisco. Two floors. Everything smelled like a wet dog. The fiction section was on the ground level. On the second Josip Novakovich was reading from his latest collection of war stories. He was a large and intense man. The back of his head looked like David Lynch's. I would've sat, listened intently, and had him autograph a copy of *Infidelities: Stories of War and Lust,* but I hadn't developed a taste for East-European Literature. *Not quite true*. I loved Gogol. Dostoevsky too.

Besides, my mission that night was to regain my death drive. According to Slavoj Žižek the death drive is not to be mistaken with the so-called 'nirvana principle'. I didn't want to simply return to a state of quiescence but to return to the state before quiescence, before my birth, before my parents' birth, before my grandparents' birth, before my great-grandparents' birth, before life, before the universe, before the big bang, before the point of no return. I wanted so desperately to turn the very fabric of that beforeness into an afterness, an ouroboros without head nor tail. To transcend transcendence, this was my concern!

In retrospect I can see that seppuku was a step in the wrong direction. '[T]he death drive stands for its exact opposite, for the dimension of the 'undead', of a spectral life which insists beyond (biological) death.' (93) I have Žižek's *The Puppet and the Dwarf* in front of me as I write. The back cover art is a portrait of himself lying next to a photo of a vagina. Born 1947. He looks his age. Like Novakovich. As these apocalyptic thoughts came to a head, the world did as well. The ground beneath me literally began to shake. A tsunami? Mild rolling. More like an aftershock. Later on I would learn it was a magnitude 6.2, with the epicentre thirty miles away. There was no damage. A few books fell. One in particular caught my eye. What is this? *The Sea Came In At Midnight* by Steve Erickson. A blue paperback. The blurb on the cover asked, 'What is missing from the world?' I silently answered, 'My absence.' Synchronicity? Fate? Destiny? I don't know. Steve Erickson lived in Los Angeles. He taught at CalArts, a school my mother and father attended. I wasn't familiar with the name. But the praise and the quotes on the cover made me feel as if I should have known it.

'Steve Erickson is a provocative visionary chronicler of a phantasmagorical america on the brink of the apocalypse... Erickson's novel is at once maddening and engrossing, unfolding like an elaborate game in which the rules are ever shifting. He's written the literary equivalent of a tsunami into which the reader must dive headlong or else risk drowning in the author's flood of dreamlike imagery and bizarre imaginings.'
–*Toronto Globe and Mail*

'Of all the millennial visions galloping... this year faster than you can say 'four horsemen', *The Sea Came In at Midnight* is likely the most challenging, and the most poetic. If you read one philosophical-doomsday kinky-sex roadtrip novel this year, make it this one.'
–*Salon*

'A major writer is in our midst. Pynchon, Nabokov, DeLillo – Steve Erickson has approached their heights.'
–*Wall Street Journal*

I was most weary of the last quote. I hated reading Pynchon, Nabokov (although *Lolita,* I will admit worked), and DeLillo, especially DeLillo. If Erickson was anything like him, forget it. But it turned out *Wall Street Journal* had its head up its ass. DeLillo was DeLillo. Erickson was always Erickson. And if any one had exceeded their heights it was him.

Twenty pages into the novel I was enthralled. I felt goose bumps. I was filled with a strange, haunted desire. People on the second floor applauded. Novakovich took some questions. *Salon* and *Toronto Globe* didn't do it justice. *The Sea Came In At Midnight*. What a strange and marvellous novel this is. It could easily serve as a sourcebook for those that are in need of an understanding of japanese paraculture and its psychic past. Although, some would argue that Erickson simply used japan as a screen for his id-projections, it had singlehandedly reignited my faith in the death drive. To hell with Plath's and Mishima's unimaginative suicides. Erickson had a bigger and better plan for me. An apocalyptic vision. Page 17. 'Almost a mile and a half down Highway 1, somewhere between Mendocino and Bodega Bay…' I would throw myself off the ocean cliffs. I would find myself by terrifying myself. I would become the fountain of blood. I would insert myself into the myth by out-mythologising the very thing that was but myth. In the end I'd hope to become an inextricable part of that 'maddening and engrossing' roar of endless waves and breaking surf. To transcend transcendence. It was to be beautiful, vast and all too amorphous.

The drive up the I-5 would be long. An interminable eight hours. The rain poured down. The orange full moon was low to the horizon and unusually large, almost pulsating. It was so bright you could make it out through the clouds. Every car and truck manœuvred around me. The high winds pushed against my small car. I felt vulnerable. But I wanted to remember every sound. Every sight. Every detail. I convinced myself that everything about that night would be frightfully important. I pondered the uncanny parallels and similitudes between the protagonist of *The Sea* and myself. We both live in LA. We both never thought we would see Tokyo. She had articles in literary journals and art magazines about Flannery O'Connor and Kathy Acker. I'd written similar articles about O'Connor and Acker. Kristin lived in the Hotel Ryu. My father's name was Ryu. Kristin never had dreams. I never had dreams. She kept a notebook. I kept a notebook. What did it all mean? All these separate parts fitting in to an intricate mosaic. Only, I had to go to the cliffs to see it for myself. To see the whole picture.

I accepted the fact that somewhere along the line my life had somehow crossed into, bled into Erickson's novel or Erickson's novel had somehow crossed into my own. Either way I couldn't go back. In Erickson's narrative 1,999 souls jumped off a Mendocino ocean cliff and it was clear that I'd be the two-thousandth soul neccesary to bring about the end of the narrative. I would have to do what the protagonist of the book could not. The earthquake at the bookstore had only confirmed the occult powers of the author. An imminent cosmic cataclysm was to be had, and I would be the final domino to fall.

Acknowledgements

Many people have assisted in various ways in the writing of this book. I should like in particular to thank my dear parents and brother Matt. This book was researched in part during the years I spent at California Institute of the Arts; I am very grateful to CalArts' CSSSA class of 2000, MFA Critical Studies class and staff and the BFA class of 2005–2007 for the inspiration and moral support. I have benefited a great deal from conversations with many CalArts faculty staff. I would particularly like to thank my mentor Matias Viegener and Steve Erickson who patiently talked me through many of the literary and anti-literary issues of the earliest drafts. As I started out on what was unfamiliar territory, Jen Hofer, Jon Wagner and Christine Wertheim gave me invaluable theoretical and philosophical directions. I am indebted to Norman Klein for his encouragement. Gina Clark assisted me with her notes, inspiring art and collaborative spirit—the book would have been poorer without her. I have also had many enlightening conversations with Bruce Bauman, John Gill, Helen Kim, Chris Kraus, Bridghe Mullins, Maggie Nelson, Matt Timmons and Dante West. I am very grateful to Janice Lee and Janet Sarbanes who read the thesis version of the manuscript and made insightful suggestions. Thanks to Laura Bunting of MOCA Library for access to the Takashi Murakami material. Additional thanks to Johnny Golding for shedding light on the magic garden. I should also like to thank Sylvère Lotringer and Eric Nakamura for living outside the categories for so many years. Lastly, thanks to all at Book Works, especially my editors Gavin Everall and Stewart Home (aka Mister Trippy)—this book would not have been possible without the catalyst, *69 THINGS TO DO WITH A DEAD PRINCESS.*

One Break, A Thousand Blows!
Maxi Kim
Semina No. 2
Published and distributed by Book Works, London

ISBN 978 1 906012 05 2

Commissioning editor: Stewart Home
Edited by Stewart Home and Gavin Everall
Designed by Fraser Muggeridge studio
Printed by Die Keure, Bruges

Book Works
19 Holywell Row
London
EC2A 4JB
www.bookworks.org.uk
tel: +44 (0)20 7247 2203

Book Works is funded by Arts Council England